I0659321

I Confess

Leopold Borstinski

SOBRIETY
PRESS

Monday, September 7, 1953

1

I READ MY newspaper much as I did most mornings in my inner sanctum, my feet resting on the corner of my desk, the paper balanced on my outstretched legs. I kept sipping from the mug of java clasped in my hand as I proceeded from back to front. First the sports, on to the funnies, and then I did my best to wade through the news stories until boredom took hold and I stared out of the window of my serviced office.

The place comprised two rooms: my inner sanctum with a couple of chairs for clients and a couch for when I needed to contemplate the complexities of a case with my eyes shut. My secretary, Sylvia, occupied the other space. She was a young blond thing whose primary tasks were to prevent riffraff from reaching the inner sanctum and to do whatever paperwork was necessary to keep the cops and the IRS off my back.

Rat-a-tat-tat on the door and she popped her head into the room; I had yet to invest in any modern technology like an intercom.

"There's a woman who wants to see you, but she won't tell me what it is all about. Are you in?"

I threw the newspaper under my desk and pulled my tie back up to my neck. Then I whipped on my jacket, which was hanging on a hatstand near a wall.

"Does she look dangerous?"

Sylvia glanced into the reception area and then returned her head to the inner sanctum.

"I wouldn't say so, although she might have a concealed weapon."

"As she will have seen you talking to me, if I were you, I'd tell her I am here and show her in."

Sylvia nodded and closed the door. Ten seconds later, it opened again, and she led in a dame wearing a fancy cream skirt suit and a wide-brimmed matching hat.

"Mr. Adkins, I need your help in a delicate matter."

"Call me Jake, all my friends do."

"You misunderstand. I don't wish to be your friend, I want to hire you as a private investigator."

I beckoned to a chair with a simple open-palmed gesture and the dame sat down. As she did so, I admired her curves, which were conveniently located in all the right places.

"Let's start from the beginning, Miss…?"

"Mrs. Avril Langchamp."

I glanced at her left hand and noticed an ill-fitting wedding band.

"Are you from around here?"

"I have lived in California all my life. My parents have French ancestry, but that isn't important."

"Then what is, Mrs. Langchamp?"

"The police arrested me last night on suspicion of murdering my husband, and I need you to prove that I did it."

I STARED AND blinked for a moment, not sure how to respond. Even back then, I'd been in the business a few years, but this was the first time a prospective client had walked into my office protesting their guilt. A standard approach was the opposite of Avril Langchamp's request.

"Would you like a coffee, Mrs. Langchamp?"

I waved my mug in the air so that she knew what I meant, but a dame wearing that quality of skirt had seen a hot drink before. Sylvia must have been listening at the door because at that moment her head appeared again.

"Sugar?"

"Cream only, please."

This gave me enough time to think through her proposition. I attempted more small talk until Sylvia sashayed out of my inner sanctum, having delivered the second mug.

"Mrs. Langchamp, are you telling me you killed your husband?"

"I have made no such claim. What I am asking you to do is find sufficient evidence I did it to convince the district attorney that they should prosecute me."

"Tell me what happened and then I'll let you know if I can take your case."

"And are our conversations protected by client privilege?"

"I'm no lawyer, so no. But our professional reputation is important enough to all of us private eyes that we don't go telling tales out of school."

"Is that your way of saying you'll keep your mouth shut if the police ask about me?"

"It means I will remain silent at least until a judge forces me to spill, and I've spent time in jail for contempt before now."

She took a sip of her coffee and winced. Sylvia had burned it again. I returned her stare and leaned back in my seat, hoping to put her at ease enough to give me her story.

⸎ ⸎

"THIS IS WHAT happened. Kole and I had an argument last night. He threatened me and I killed him."

"Kole is your husband?"

"Of course."

"Did you phone the cops or can we thank some leading light of the citizenry?"

"Oh, as soon as I knew he was dead, I dialed their number."

"Did you confess?"

"I'm not a Catholic, Mr. Adkins."

"Please call me Jake."

She bristled for a second. Her sort like to ensure there is distance between themselves and the hired help. What she forgot was that I hadn't agreed to take the case at that point.

"What were you arguing about?"

"Huh?"

"You said that you and Kole had a disagreement. What was it about?"

"That doesn't matter right now. My problem is that the DA has already informed the police that he's not minded to prosecute me. I want you to change his opinion."

"And tell me again why you want to be prosecuted."

"I never told you in the first place. I will pay you for your time and your effort. I will not fund you to interrogate me. All you need to know is that I want you to convince the police that I should have my day in court."

This was when I had to perform multiple calculations in my head within a matter of seconds. My usual fee back then was fifty dollars, but this was a most unusual situation.

"My rate is a hundred bucks."

"No, it is not."

My cheeks heated up.

"Did you not get my name out of the phone directory?"

"Not at all. Inspector Granger gave me your number and let me know what I should pay you."

"I must remember to thank Lou for the referral. He told you I was a seventy-five-dollar dick, right?"

"Not quite. Fifty, but I will go as far as seventy if it'll help you keep your attention on my case."

For that much money, I'd watch my mother taking a shower.

"Works for me."

"How long do you reckon it will take?"

"That's hard for me to say without starting my investigation."

"I'll give you cash to last until Friday. If you haven't done the job by then, I shall find someone else who can."

2

THE FIRST PLACE to go was over to the precinct where the dame had been taken when she was arrested. It was a building I knew well. I could pretend this was because I visited on business so frequently, but I'd seen the inside of one of its cells once too often for my liking.

I sighed as I pulled into the West Los Angeles police station on the corner of Purdue and Iowa. If I didn't know better, I'd say the bricks recognized me and readied themselves for the trouble that I ordinarily brought to the joint.

At reception, I asked the desk clerk to tell Inspector Granger that he had a visitor.

"Who wants him?"

"I do. I just told you."

"What's your name, Mac?"

"You don't have to worry. Lou knows me."

"If you want to meet Granger, then give me your name. If not, get out of here, you bum."

"Tell him Jake Adkins has come calling."

A dagger stare from the flatfoot behind the desk and he instructed that I wait a moment, and he'd find out if Lou was in. Two minutes later and the big lunk waddled toward me and thrust his hand into mine.

"Good to see you, Jake. How's tricks?"

"Not bad. Can we go to your office? I've got some business I need to discuss with you."

His eyebrows shot to the top of his forehead until he recalled the referral to Langchamp and he led me to the second floor where the homicide division was located. We sat down at his desk, which was to one side of the vast number of detectives focused on the unlawfully dead of Los Angeles.

"WHAT'S HAPPENING, JAKE?"

"You arrested and released my client last night and I want to find out what's her story."

Lou leaned back in his chair and smiled.

"Who are we talking about?"

"Don't be coy. How many women did you take into custody in the last twenty-four hours?"

"Avril Langchamp is a piece of work. Unquestionably."

"Why do you say that, Lou?"

"Killed her husband stone dead and barely broke into a sweat."

"Never come across shock, Inspector?"

"That's as may be, but when officers arrived at the scene, her hands were covered in blood and Mr. Langchamp lay on the floor as deceased as he could be."

"She says the DA won't press charges."

"Yep. The neighbors heard a commotion and called in the complaint. And not for the first time."

"So this was a domestic dispute gone bad?"

"That's what it appears like."

"You have your doubts, Lou?"

"If the district attorney doesn't want to prosecute, who am I to say otherwise? There was a history of neighbor complaints and if you pop to the morgue, then you'll discover the guy was a thickset monster. I wonder what she saw in him because they weren't together for his good looks."

"It takes all sorts to make a world, Lou."

"Sure, Jake. But you've met the woman. She could have had her choice of any man in the city, but she chose a lunk like that."

I nodded.

"Perhaps she admired him for his wallet and not his physical features."

"Perhaps you're right."

"Apart from a history of shouting loud enough for somebody next door to hear, why won't the DA proceed?"

"He reckons that Kole Langchamp must have provoked her because of the disparity in their physical presence. Besides, Jake. What jury is going to believe she is anything but innocent when she simpers her way through the court proceedings? If she takes the stand, one teardrop will make the jurors putty in the defense's hands."

I ignored Lou's comment. He was a cop and not a poet, but he had a point. However, that didn't explain why the broad was so keen to have her day in court. To me, it seemed like she'd dodged a bullet. She has a fight with her gorilla of a husband. It turns ugly. She grabs a knife and stabs him until he is dead. End of.

Mrs. Langchamp was right, though. She was paying me to do her bidding and not to second-guess her reasons.

"Lou, what would it take for the DA to reconsider his position and call a grand jury?"

"Hard evidence that there was more to the escapade than self-defense."

"And you've given up on the case?"

"If there's no one to prosecute, why should I spend more time on nothing?"

I nodded again. The guy was a clear ten years older than me and had been on the force since he left school. He'd helped me out of a few scrapes over the years, and landed me in trouble too. No matter what people said about Inspector Lou Granger, he had a good heart. I was certain of that much.

"Would you like a beer?"

THE WAY I figured, Lou was his own man, and when you took him away from his precinct and the ears of any nearby police officers, the guy told you what he believed. It was one of the reasons I liked the fella in the first place. He was the kind of cop who would make sure the cuffs weren't too tight when he arrested you.

With two beers standing tall in front of us in O'Malley's, a bar down the road from the station, Lou glanced left and right before taking the glass in one of his mammoth hands and slurping down his first mouthful. I took a sip and waited.

"The dame's a strange lady, Jake."

"How'd you mean?"

"For starters, she murders her husband and calls the police."

"I figured that's what every upright citizen is meant to do."

"You're right, but people who plug their husbands with a kitchen knife are not that upright."

"Perhaps after the act, she realized what she had done. Came to, you might say, from the mist that had engulfed her."

"Maybe so, but why do you believe she's so keen for the DA to step in? You should have been here last night, Jake. She talked like a woman who had been on the receiving end of one too many beatings —verbal or otherwise."

"Are you telling me she had a change of heart overnight?"

"I'm saying nothing. If the DA doesn't want anything more to do with the dame, then neither do I, nor any of the men. Just remember that if you dig up anything, then you'll make all of us cops appear real bad. I might not look the other way in the future should you park in front of a fire hydrant."

"Let me get this straight, Lou. If I do my job and my client is convicted, which is ridiculous in itself, then the local force will give me a hard time?"

"You take everything so personally, Jake. It's not about you. We have professional pride and don't like gumshoes making us look bad."

"If I get my own client convicted?"

"Pretty much. Yep."

I took another swig of my drink to clear my head. Was I about to incur the wrath of the West Los Angeles police department? The other item I hadn't factored in was the scale of the impact finding my own client guilty might have on future business.

"Lou, do you believe I should drop the case?"

"Is she paying you well?"

"I doubled my rate, and she didn't gouge me when we haggled."

"That says a lot, Jake, if you think about it."

"Now you're getting inside my head. You have a vested interest in my failure and want me to walk away."

"I was messing with you just now. If you gather enough evidence so the DA can convict her, then we all come up smelling of roses. If you don't, then she's still paid you. No harm, no foul."

I finished my beer and threw some greenbacks on the bar before we both left the joint.

"What are you going to do?"

"Hop over to Langchamp's pad and check it out. You're right, I've got nothing to lose and if I succeed, I'll be the first private eye to throw his own client into jail."

3

THE LANGCHAMP RESIDENCE was much like any other house on the street. Its only distinguishing feature was the police tape stuck across the front door. If it wasn't for that clue, I'd have been hard pushed to guess which one of the buildings before me had been home to a gruesome death.

My job was to get the DA to agree that Mrs. Langchamp's actions were so heinous that she must be put on trial and then her attorney would convince a jury that she did not do it. To be honest, I didn't understand why she was putting herself through this, only to come out the other side unscathed. But she was paying me enough, so I didn't have to care.

First, I took a tour of the plot. The backyard was in a reasonable condition, but the grass hadn't been cut for a few weeks. There was a hut at the far end of the yard. I peered through its window and spotted only spiders' webs and horticultural equipment. I tried the door handle just in case, but it was rusted shut. At least it saved me the bother of fighting the insects that had turned the shed into their home.

As I headed toward the rear of the house, a rustling of the second-floor curtains on my right caught my attention. Nothing I hadn't seen before. Neighbors tell themselves that they want to keep to their own little kingdoms and not pay no never mind to anyone else, but as soon as a stranger rears his ugly head within five hundred feet, you can bet your last cent that some busybody will stick their nose in.

Up at the house, I checked the back door handle, which opened with no effort on my part. I was prepared to take out a tool from Old Faithful, the special wallet I always kept in my jacket pocket, but there was no need today. Crouching, I slipped under the police tape and entered.

I ONLY HAD enough time to stare at the kitchen counter before there was a knock on the front door, and then a moment later, the doorbell rang. Now was not the time to be playing house guest, so I slipped out of the back and scurried to the side of the building to get a better view of the caller.

She wore a housecoat and I couldn't help but notice the red sequined slippers on her feet. Perhaps she was a witch from Oz. This seemed less likely a couple of minutes later when I started talking to her.

"Hi, who are you?"

"More to the point, what are you doing poking around at the Langchamp residence?"

I eyed her up and down as we stood near the front of the house. As my gaze lingered over her body, she tightened the cord around her waist. Mid-thirties, blue eyes, long brown hair.

"I'm looking into what happened here on Sunday night."

Her shoulders lowered.

"I thought you might have been a burglar."

"If you believed that, you should have phoned the police and not come knocking on the door."

I beamed to take the edge off my admonishment and she smiled back.

"My name is Jack Adkins, but my friends call me Jake. And you are...?"

"Gladys Blake. I live next door."

She was my curtain rustler: it stood to reason.

"Did you hear or see anything on Sunday night, Mrs. Blake?"

"And you can call me Gladys. Would you like a coffee and we can talk about it inside, Jake?"

She shivered, and I realized she must have been quite cold. I nodded and followed her to the street and along to her house.

———   ———

THE PLACE WAS filled with the sounds of children playing. Two tykes flew past me and back upstairs. They were too quick for me to figure out if they were boys or girls.

"Sorry about the mess, but with those critters under my feet, I hardly have time to clear up after them."

"No need to apologize, Gladys. They seem like mighty-fine little 'uns."

"How kind of you to say so."

She led me into the kitchen and bustled about with a coffee pot that she'd taken out of a wall-mounted cupboard. Back in her own lair, she was more relaxed and allowed the cord of her housecoat to undo.

"What were the Langchamps like as neighbors, Gladys?"

"They weren't much of a bother. Kept themselves apart from the rest of the street."

"Is there a close community here?"

I glanced round as though I could see through walls to the other inhabitants of the road.

"Those of us with kids stick together, if you know what I mean."

"Were the Langchamps as blessed as you are?"

Gladys smiled at the compliment. I figure I don't care what lies I tell if I find out what I need to know. For all her talk of family, this woman wasn't interested in her brats that much otherwise she'd scream at them to stop their yowling.

"No, AJ and Kole only had each other."

"AJ?"

"Avril Langchamp. She preferred not to stress her foreign name. Not everyone is as enlightened as some of us."

With that pronouncement, Gladys walked over to the kitchen table and bent down to place a coffee mug in front of me. Her housecoat was loose enough for me to wonder whether she was wearing any pajamas, which didn't appear to be the case no matter how hard I stared.

"Did the couple have any problems that you knew of?"

"You mean if we ignore how small-minded some people are?"

"Yes, I'm open to almost anything, so you can tell me what you thought of AJ and Kole."

Her eyes widened a touch as I said that, but she remained leaning with her back against the kitchen sink with both knees visible where the housecoat had fallen away.

"We'd hear the occasional shouting of an evening, but they were married, so what do you expect?"

"Were their altercations ever loud enough for you to make out what they said?"

"Only when we were on the patio and most of the time, it sounded like they were arguing over money. But don't get me wrong, this was only a handful of times since they moved in."

"How long ago was that?"

Gladys thought for a moment and I couldn't decide if she was recalling the day the Langchamps arrived or whether she was considering how much more of her body she was going to show me. There wasn't a huge amount left to my imagination.

"Six months, more or less."

"And did they have many visitors?"

"I wouldn't know. You make me sound as though I spend my days checking on my neighbors."

"Not at all, Gladys. It's just that you have a good eye for detail and I'd be grateful for any insights you can offer me."

I took a glug from my coffee to give her a chance to collect herself. The pot had only been on the hotplate for a few seconds, but the drink was burned. Judging by her behavior with me, I guessed Mr. Blake wasn't interested in Gladys for her culinary skills.

"You are very kind, Jake. I noticed they held a few pool parties at the weekend, but nothing too raucous."

"Did you see who attended these get-togethers?"

"Not at all. We have a hedge between our place and theirs, although there was one night…"

Gladys's voice faded away as she recalled something I couldn't see. I remained silent and waited for her to return to the room.

"I was putting the kids to bed upstairs, and I looked out. There was a noise from next door, splashing."

"They don't have a pool though?"

"No, but they do have a hot tub. And a man and a woman were in it, and they were naked."

"Not the Langchamps?"

"No, because Kole handed cocktails to the two in the tub."

"Was AJ anywhere to be seen?"

"Not from my vantage point."

"Then what happened?"

"I kissed my two goodnight and popped downstairs."

"And you saw nothing else?"

"No, not a thing. Is it important?"

"You never know in my line of work, Gladys. By the way, were you the kind neighbor who phoned the police?"

"Me? Oh no, whatever gave you that idea?"

I shrugged and finished the dregs of my coffee to give myself something to do because I was certain there was more that the woman had to offer.

"Would you like to see the rest of the house, Jake?"

"Why would I want to do that?"

"Because we have the same layout as the Langchamps and I guess you can't walk through their crime scene."

"You make a good point, Gladys."

She smiled, and we wandered around the first floor until we looped back to the stairs. Up we trotted and Gladys showed me the kids' bedrooms. "AJ used these as a study and a spare room instead."

Then we poked our heads into the bathroom and she led me to the last room, which I assumed was the master bedroom. She leaned against the door jamb and her housecoat parted ways a little above her knees. She exhaled and puffed out her not-inconsiderable chest. The housecoat separated further.

"Would you like to check out my chamber, Jake?"

"If it's worth seeing, Gladys."

"I've not had any complaints yet."

She sashayed into her room and I followed, loosening my tie. There she was, sitting on the bed, her robe had fallen around her hips and she was beautiful.

"Your kids?"

"Close the door because they know better than to barge in here when it's shut."

"Do you entertain often?"

"You ask a lot of questions for a man standing dressed in front of a naked woman."

She was right. I threw my jacket onto the floor and unbuttoned my cuffs. A slam jolted me into reality and I stared at Gladys, who had whipped her housecoat tight around her body.

"Hi, Patrick. You're home early."

By the time she'd completed that statement, my jacket had returned to cover my torso, and I looked askance at her. She placed a solitary finger against her lips to keep me quiet and bustled downstairs.

"Would you like a coffee, darling?"

The muffled response must have been positive because Gladys declared her intention to go to the kitchen, which was my cue to exit the premises by any means necessary.

4

I SCURRIED OUT of the front door and hoped Patrick was occupied enough by his libidinous wife not to detect my exit. I finished putting on my jacket on the stoop and hustled past the Langchamp residence to the other neighbors.

A rat-a-tat on the next door and the lady of the house appeared.

"We're not buying."

"That's good because I have nothing to sell you. Instead, I'm investigating Mr. Langchamp's death."

"Oh, I'd been told AJ did him in."

"Where did you hear that?"

The woman shrugged and eyed me up and down. I smiled and tipped my hat, hoping that would appease her.

"Who did you say you were?"

"I didn't. My name is Jack Adkins, but my friends call me Jake."

I flashed my PI badge too because nobody reads the words under the shiny gold lump and makes the incorrect assumption that somehow I am a cop.

"Would you like to come inside?"

"Thank you, ma'am. That'd be mighty fine."

She led me to the living room and pointed at an armchair. Isabelle Henson relaxed into her couch and sipped at a glass of water she'd poured for herself before my arrival. She was polite enough to offer me a seat but not so well-mannered as to give me a drink.

"We were all so surprised, Mr. Adkins."

"Call me Jake."

"Shocking. And to think it all happened just a few feet from where we're sitting."

I pondered the prospect of languishing in a room while a woman snuffed the life out of her husband next door. It'd put me off my second cocktail, for sure.

"Did you hear what went on?"

"No, not at all. Mr. Henson and I watched television and then we retired to bed."

"What time was that?"

"Around ten, I guess."

"And, Mrs. Henson, what were the Langchamps like as neighbors?"

"They kept themselves to themselves."

"Any parties?"

"Avril took advantage of the summer months to host the occasional gathering, but not what you'd call excessive."

"Were you or your husband invited to any of them?"

"One or two, I suppose."

"Anything interesting happen?"

"Whatever do you mean?"

"Nothing in particular. I'd just like to get a sense of what these parties were like."

"People stood around, drank cocktails, talked to each other, and left. I wouldn't say anything happened of any note."

The Langchamps' neighbors had different experiences of the same get-togethers. Perhaps Gladys had let her imagination run away with her. Or Isabelle had something to hide.

"So everything was peachy between husband and wife?"

"That is not my place to say."

"What's that supposed to mean, Isabelle?"

"You asked if we heard anything the night of the…"

"Murder?"

"Yes. And we didn't hear a thing that evening."

"But on other occasions?"

"Occasionally, we discerned raised voices."

"Above the sound of the television?"

"Sometimes. Rarely, mind. But now and again."

"Could you make out what they were arguing about?"

"I am not the sort of person who eavesdrops."

"I'm sure not, Isabelle."

"Money was the principal topic. AJ would remind Kole that he needed to be careful with it."

"Was he profligate?"

A blank expression from Isabelle.

"I don't know about that, Jake. How could I?"

Then it was my turn to look blankly at her until I realized she had misunderstood my question.

"Sorry, Isabelle. Would you say that Kole spent a lot of green?"

"Oh!" She giggled. "I was thinking of something totally different."

I chuckled back to pretend to share the joke, although there was a world of difference between a prophylactic and profligate. And there was nothing funny about either.

"They had no fancy car, and he didn't wear expensive clothes. Is that what you meant?"

"Yeah, that sort of thing."

"Did you call the police that night?"

"No. I told you we didn't hear or see anything. Well, not until the blue flashing lights and sirens appeared outside."

"And one last question, Isabelle. On the day of the murder, did you see any unusual activity?"

"Not from here, we couldn't. You'd need to ask the Frosts over the road."

I thanked Isabelle for her help and tried to show myself out, although she insisted on following me the ten feet. Perhaps she reckoned I would steal the silverware.

I DECIDED TO take a different tack with the Frost residence, especially as I was thirsty from watching Isabelle consume most of a glass of water in front of me. At one point, I reckon she smacked her lips to reflect the pleasure she received from that clear draft of liquid refreshment. Or maybe it was my imagination. Rat-a-tat-tat.

Despite the time it took for somebody to come to the door, I knew someone was in from the general hubbub emanating from the house.

"Mrs. Frost?"

"Are you with the police?"

I flashed my badge to answer that question. Before I'd switched on my charm, she had already invited me in.

"Terrible business, Inspector…?"

"I'm not an inspector, but I am investigating the murder that took place yesterday. The name is Jack Adkins, but my friends call me Jake."

"Ashley Frost. Charmed, I'm sure."

She fluttered her eyelids at me and showed me into the living room. Gladys was right: these houses had identical layouts; only the colors on the walls and the furnishings inside made them distinguishable from each other.

A coffee table separated two couches. I sat on one, while Ashley chose the other. Before we began, I had an important matter to attend to.

"Sorry to impose, but do you have a glass of water or even a coffee? I've been talking all morning and my throat is getting sore."

"Of course, officer. Sounds like you'd prefer a java."

"Just call me Jake, and that would be mighty fine. Thank you."

The trick is never to say you are with the police as that constitutes fraud in every state of the union. But the words I use are laid out so that the hearer can reach their own, often erroneous, conclusion. It helps me get through the day that much easier.

Ashley returned with a tray upon which were a pot of coffee, two cups, and a plate of cookies. I accepted both the drink and something to eat and thanked her for her effort.

"So, how can I help you, Jake?"

"How well did you know the Langchamps?"

"Nobody on this part of the street lives in each other's pockets, but we knew them enough to talk to them if we bumped into AJ or Kole in the front yard."

"You weren't any closer than that? I've been informed they held summer parties. Were you ever invited?"

"No, some might have been, but not us."

"Did they cause you any problems? With parking, for example?"

"Whoever described them as parties must get out less than we do. There'd be a handful of couples there. Three or four at most."

"Oh. Perhaps they were louder if you lived next door."

Ashley raised an eyebrow to indicate her views of either Isabelle or Gladys. I wondered what happened between them all to create this tension.

"Do you know if they were having any difficulties, Ashley?"

"We weren't best buddies. We wouldn't have found out about any problems between the couple."

"And did they get many visitors, apart from their weekend gatherings?"

"No more than anybody else, I'd say. I mean, people would show up two or three times a week."

"How long would they stay?"

"Jake, it's not like we stared out of the window and took notes on their comings and goings."

"Of course not."

I glanced across the street from my seat with its perfect view of the Langchamps' entrance. Even if I had sat on Ashley's couch, I reckoned it'd be easy to keep a watchful eye on the Langchamp residence.

"A person might hear the clunk of a car door shutting and glance up once in a while, but nothing more than that."

"Were the clunks quite far apart?"

"Now that you ask, I wouldn't say so. I wasn't staring at the clock, but most of the time they'd be in there for less than thirty minutes."

"And did you spot the same individuals return, or were they always different?"

"Mainly the same, I suppose."

She glanced down as if she had reflected on what she was telling me and realized what a lonely life she and her husband had led. They spent their nights watching other people out there in the world.

"Would you recognize them again?"

"I don't know about that. It was evening or nighttime and the light wasn't that good."

"One final question: did you call the police the night of the murder?"

"No, we didn't."

"You've been exceedingly helpful, Ashley. Thank you for your time and those terrific cookies. You sure are a great baker."

Her cheeks glowed and her eyes lowered to her lap again. With bupkis of insight from Ashley, I figured the next thing to do was to get a proper look inside the Langchamp home.

I tried AJ's front door as soon as I left, but there was no reply. For a moment, I considered making my way to the rear of the house and checking the place out again in private, but I knew I needed to speak with Mrs. Langchamp more than I felt the need to rifle through her drawers. Instead, I decided to grab a bite to eat and come back in a couple of hours.

5

AS I WALKED up the drive on South Fifth Plaza, a black sedan was parked in front of the garage.

"I hope you don't mind this uninvited guest, Mrs. Langchamp."

Her stare burned into my soul, but she smiled and gestured me in. Without an offer of a drink, let alone a cookie, we got down to business as soon as I made myself comfortable in the living room.

"What did you want to tell me, Mr. Adkins?"

"Jake, remember."

Another stare to show she was less interested in recalling my first name and more concerned with getting a full report from me.

"Your neighbors didn't hear or see anything on the night of the…"

"Murder, Jake."

"Yeah. We need to find some evidence to convince the DA that you were home and that something justified the killing."

"The district attorney has my confession."

"But that's not enough, otherwise he'd have charged you and I wouldn't be sitting here right now."

She nodded and pondered for a moment.

"Are you telling me I need the opposite of an alibi? You'd prefer it if somebody had seen me kill Kole?"

I stifled a laugh.

"In an ideal world, Mrs. Langchamp."

"We live a long way from a place like that, don't we?"

The time we spent in my office did not prepare me for her withering looks. She had given off the appearance of a damsel in distress when we first met.

"Mrs. Langchamp, perhaps if you told me the circumstances of Kole's death, then I might figure out where to find the evidence you crave."

"You want me to do your job for you?"

"I'd like to have a little more to go on if I am to succeed. When you keep me in the dark, I'm likely to walk into walls."

"I'm not comfortable with you prying into my personal life."

"Nobody is, Mrs. Langchamp, but the DA believes Kole's was a justified homicide and sees no benefit in prosecuting you. While I cannot imagine why you would want to step foot in a courtroom that the DA doesn't have interest in you entering, this is what you have told me is our goal. For me to assist you, I must understand why you killed your husband…"

She sighed and raised her eyes to the ceiling as if in despair.

"Forgive me for asking."

"Would it help you if I said that he hit me and mistreated me?"

"That'd be a start."

"Unfortunately for you, he didn't, Jake."

Now it was my turn to sigh. What was the dame's problem? For a woman who wanted to be found guilty of manslaughter, she was making it hard for me to do my job.

"Are you aware of anything we can use to change the DA's mind?"

"If I was sitting on that, I wouldn't be paying you seventy dollars a day, now would I?"

"I reckon not."

We stared blankly at each other until Mrs. Langchamp stood up and busied herself at a sideboard on the other side of the room. In a moment, she was back, but despite my best hopes, she was not clutching a signed declaration by Kole that he had provoked his wife to murder him.

"Is there anything else you can tell me, Jake?"

"Some of your neighbors didn't appreciate your summer gatherings by the hot tub."

"Never mind. I doubt if there'll be too many more of those happening."

"Because Kole is dead or due to the weather?"

"Don't be insolent. My husband is dead. Why would I party?"

"You might want your friends near you at a time like this."

A quizzical expression took over her face. Then a smile.

"Those people were clients, not friends."

"What line of work were you and your husband involved in?"

"Real estate. We'd schmooze the high rollers hoping a martini or two might swing more business our way."

"Was it a successful strategy?"

"Every time."

A gleam appeared in the corner of her eye and I felt queasy.

"Do you mind if I go to the bathroom?"

"THE BEDROOM IS no longer a crime scene, if you want to take a look."

"Have the police dusted for prints?"

"Some bumbling oaf made a mess of my surfaces, yes."

Mrs. Langchamp wanted everything and gave away nothing, apart from my upfront fee. My first stop was the bathroom and, after I flushed, I checked out the medicine cabinet.

The contents were the usual collection of items, other than what was missing. Not a single piece of female apparel. Mrs. Langchamp did not frequent this room on a regular basis, but it was filled with a razor and other shaving equipment, so Kole had made himself at home here.

This begged the question of where Avril powdered her nose. I slunk along the landing and popped my head around the door that still had a fleck of police tape attached to the jamb.

There was a pile of bedding on the floor and the acrid stench of vomit hung in the air. Had Kole thrown up or Mrs. Langchamp? Hard to tell. I imagined the two of them in hand-to-hand combat and then scrubbed that idea out of my mind. Given her frame, there was no way she would have been able to subdue Kole for a moment, let alone long enough to squeeze the life out of him.

Only one pillow lay around, and then it struck me. There was only a single bed in the guest bedroom. Mr. and Mrs. Langchamp were sleeping in separate rooms. Why had she not mentioned that? In fact, now that I considered it, she had sidestepped offering a description of how she had killed Kole at all.

I bent down to search for any evidence the cops had missed. Whoever had cleaned up the mess left by Kole's body hadn't bothered looking under the bed. There was still a pool of drying blood and what appeared to be a steel box.

"Discover anything interesting, Jake?"

I almost banged my head on the bedstead in response to Mrs. Langchamp's voice. She sure was good at sneaking up on a fella.

"There's a case under there."

"Kole kept some papers in it. Cheaper than using a safe."

"Uh-huh. I know this might be painful for you, but would you please talk me through what happened on Sunday night?"

"If I must. I don't understand how that is going to help you find any evidence."

"It'll give me a better idea of where to search, Mrs. Langchamp."

"Then let's at least go back downstairs and you can fix us some drinks."

I PLACED TWO martinis down on the coasters that Mrs. Langchamp had provided and then I waited. She took a sip and sighed.

"Kole and I were comfortable with each other, but not happy. He had an unpleasant tendency to anger and somehow the things I said to him made him angry all too often."

"Had you considered leaving him?"

"Where would I go and what could I do? No, besides, I believe that marriage is for life."

"Are you sure you're not Catholic?"

She scowled before she continued.

"Over the last few weeks, I had mentioned to Kole that it'd be nice to start a family, but he wasn't keen."

"Is that the reason you two argued so loudly that your neighbors could hear?"

"It was a major bone of contention, Jake. And the more I spoke of it to Kole, the more entrenched he became in not wanting any children. But a woman can't undo what is in her heart and I persisted in trying to win him over."

"Forgive me for asking, Mrs. Langchamp, but you and Kole weren't sharing a bedroom. How did…?"

"That happened Sunday. He told me that his resistance to having a child was nothing to do with how he felt about families. He said he no longer loved me."

Another sigh and a tear fell onto her lap. A second followed and then a torrent. I stepped over and offered her my handkerchief, which she took, dabbing at her eyes until the crying abated.

"Kole moved his things into the guest bedroom in the afternoon and I prepared our dinner. Everything was calm, but there was still tension in the air, as you can imagine. After we ate, we sat in the living room and he hit the Scotch. He was always an unpleasant drunk and Sunday night was no exception."

"He attacked you?"

"Yes, he lumbered into the kitchen as I was doing the washing up and accused me of trapping him in the marriage. I had no idea what he meant, but it didn't matter. He came at me and I grabbed a knife to protect myself. When he glimpsed the blade, he turned tail and ran into the guest room, screaming that he was going to leave me. I rushed upstairs to make him stay."

"Then what happened?"

"I'm not too sure, Jake. He lunged at me and I had to defend myself. Without thinking, I'd kept the knife in my hand from the kitchen. When he attacked me, I swung the knife in front of me to protect myself. He fell to the floor and I got scared. Terror took over me and I stabbed him again."

"You called the police, though?"

"If you say so. I don't remember."

"Mrs. Langchamp, I have to tell you I am not surprised that the DA doesn't want to prosecute you. What you've just described to me is a classic case of self-defense."

"Call me AJ, now that you've heard the lowest point in my existence."

"AJ, the guy attacked you and you saved your own life."

"Jake, that can't be right. I'm pregnant and I must be guilty because I have murdered the father of my child."

6

SPENCER LOWBRIDGE REEKED of formaldehyde and I wondered when was the last time he had seen his feet. To say the man was rotund would have been an understatement. The boys in the medical examiner's office joked that he enjoyed too much linguini, but I knew the real reason. Lou told me the guy had a rare disease that made him bloated and no doubt dead before he was forty.

"Hi, Spencer."

"Hey, Jake. What are you doing here?"

"I was driving by and thought I'd drop in."

He looked at me and rolled his eyes to the heavens.

"So you aren't in the least bit interested in an early sight of the Kole Langchamp file?"

"I had no idea that was on your schedule, Spencer."

"Lou told you, I assume."

"He might have mentioned it to me in passing."

"Nice try, Jake. Nobody ever comes here unless they want to know about a cadaver. The last time I had a casual visitor, they'd taken a wrong turn at the lights."

"Well, now that he's appeared in conversation, do you have anything for me?"

"Not yet. I haven't sent my report over to Lou, so you can't possibly see the findings before he's cast an eye over the paperwork."

This wasn't going the way I'd hoped. Spencer should just tell me what I needed to know, and I could escape the aroma of death and turn tail and leave. That was not to be.

"I've already spoken with Lou, which is how I knew you were performing the autopsy. If you give me your views, that'll save me shoe leather when I hustle over to Lou and harangue him until he tells me what I need to know."

Although I doubted it would work, I added a hangdog expression. Spencer took a magnifying glass to the eyeball of his latest cadaver. I guessed this was to make me feel queasy and want to leave him alone, but I had fought in Korea and seen far worse than was on offer in a Los Angeles morgue.

"Lou told me that the deceased had been stabbed. Was that the cause of death?"

Spencer looked up and smiled.

"I forgot how persistent you are, Jake."

"When I'm paid to find answers, I ask questions until my job is done."

Spencer placed his magnifying glass down on a tray and sidled over to a pile of folders lying on his desk. He rifled through them for a moment and stopped at one smack in the middle. Next, he skimmed through the pages to remind himself of the content and threw the folder back down. That counted as filing for Spencer Lowbridge.

"Yes, Kole Langchamp was stabbed six times. There was a bruise to the back of his skull, no doubt caused when he bumped his head as he fell."

"Did the bump get him or the knife attack?"

"First, I didn't say there was a knife, only that stabbing took place. All the incisions landed in his chest area, two to the heart, three in the lungs and one caught a rib."

"Frenzied?"

"It's hard for me to offer a firm conclusion. Almost all were deep intrusions, so it is safe to assume there was a reasonable swing with each assault, especially if the chief suspect is a woman."

"I never told you that my client was female."

"There was no need. I might only deal with the aftermath of a murder, but I know the first suspect is the spouse."

"Spencer, are you asking me if my client is Mrs. Langchamp?"

"Not at all. You wouldn't tell me if I asked. Private eyes like to hide behind client privilege, even though they have none."

He snorted his derision out of his nose.

"Jake, I know that the Langchamp widow is your client because Lou told me to expect you."

"That doesn't make her my paycheck."

"Not necessarily, but Lou also explained how the DA has already dropped the case, subject to my findings, even though she admitted her guilt when officers arrived on the scene."

"Was she that quick to confess?"

"Apparently so."

I mulled that thought over for a minute while Spencer returned to investigating the skin of the corpse in front of him.

"Did you reach a conclusion about what kind of blade was used?"

"Yes, a kitchen knife, very much like the one that they found in the bedroom next to the body."

"Thanks, Spencer."

"You're welcome. Don't leave it so long before visiting next time."

"I'll try my best."

7

I HIGHTAILED IT back to the office. There was a bottle of Scotch in my bottom drawer that had my name on it to take the taste of the morgue from my mouth. Two shots later and the stench of the mortuary had dissipated from my memory.

A glance at my newspaper told me I should throw it in the trash, but that was Sylvia's job in the morning. I sure was lucky that she answered the ad I placed in the local paper. She was a girl who had curves in all the right places and also knew the correct order of the letters in the alphabet.

That reminded me that Sylvia had been begging me to find all the receipts I'd left lying around for the last month. She believed the IRS would swoop into our building without a moment's hesitation and subject us to an invasive tax audit.

I yanked out the pieces of paper stuffed into my pants pockets and threw them onto my desk. Evidence of every meal and taxi ride languished in front of me, goading me to recall why I had bought that dinner or gone on that trip. The good news is that Sylvia kept impeccable records of my comings and goings so that she could piece together my life whenever the paperwork demanded it.

This made me sit back in my chair and swivel from side to side as I concentrated my efforts on remembering every detail of what my secretary looked like. The scent of her perfume and the shape of her legs as her skirt swished around her ankles. Sometimes I'd catch sight of a calf as she sat on the other side of my desk to take dictation. Then the clatter of the keys on her typewriter would float in the air before she'd sashay over to me for a signature.

Another shot of Scotch slapped me out of my reverie and I began the dull task of sifting through my drawers in search of other pieces of tax-oriented paper. The pile on the desk was now sufficiently high that I forced myself to deal with it.

Until a minute ago, I might have convinced myself that I could sweep it off my desk onto the floor hoping it would somehow vanish with no effort from me. But I had to go through each one and make sure it was associated with a case.

Sylvia checked not only the dates, but she knew me well enough to spot something which was not tax deductible. Second only to her fear of a spontaneous IRS investigation was anxiety relating to getting caught with a wrongful submission.

As I waded through the tedium caused by her nervousness toward the IRS, I allowed my mind to wander again, back to Sylvia. The girl was not the brightest star in the sky, but she had a good heart and a fine rib cage. And she could type, file, and handle herself in front of the clients. She had been with me since I moved to LA after my business partner, Ed Schwartz, died. But that's another story.

I SNEEZED AND jerked forward, almost impaling myself on the edge of my desk. Several receipts flew into the air and landed on the floor. I swore under my breath and kneeled down to pick the damn things up. Having secured them all in one hand, I dragged myself upright and flopped back onto my swivel chair.

Why the extreme reaction to a normal bodily function? I must have dozed off for a second under the influence of the Scotch and my boredom dealing with those receipts. Another glass and I was wide awake again. Then I vowed to myself to spend the next fifteen minutes focused on sorting out the remaining pieces of paper, otherwise it'd be midnight before I was done.

I Confess

To celebrate the completion of the task, I poured myself a healthy measure, put my feet up on the corner of the desk, and sank back into the comfort of my leather seat. This gave me another opportunity to muse over Sylvia.

She wasn't the sharpest tool in the box, but though she lacked in smarts, she had chutzpah in spades. The girl treated the richest man in Los Angeles and the boy who shined his shoes in the same way. And that was one of the many aspects that attracted me to her. Now, I had never made a move on her, you understand, but that didn't stop me from viewing from afar.

AT THAT MOMENT, the door to the office suite creaked open, and I grabbed the gun from my jacket on instinct. Then the handle turned, and I raised my arm straight and pointed my piece at whoever was about to enter my room.

Sylvia let out a shriek and I hurriedly put the revolver by my side and slumped back into my chair.

"Sorry about that. I wasn't expecting you and thought the worst."

I searched in my bottom drawer, found a second glass, and poured a finger of Scotch for Sylvia, who took the drink and sipped as soon as the whiskey was in her hand.

"It's all right, Jake, but you sure scared me. You shouldn't go around pointing that thing at people."

I chose not to explain that the purpose of owning a handgun was to aim it at folk, or it wouldn't be much of a weapon, but I decided not to labor its advantages.

"As lovely as it is to see you, what are you doing here?"

"I was walking down the street and spotted that your light was on, so I popped in to find out if I could help with anything."

"You were passing this building in the evening?"

She blinked and sighed.

"Not that it's any of your business, but my boyfriend and I ate at the new Italian around the corner."

For no reason, my heart sank when Sylvia mentioned a man in her life.

"How was the food?"

"The linguini was great, and Joe said the steak was mighty fine."

"I'll check it out some time."

"You should."

"But if you were walking home from a restaurant, why visit here instead of being with your fella? Did you leave him in the lobby?"

"You ask the best questions, Jake."

"It's my job."

She covered her mouth with her hand and sniggered at me.

"I broke up with him and couldn't face the awkward silence on the journey home. You were a good excuse to end the evening."

"Sorry about that, Sylvia. Remember, I'm here if you need a shoulder to cry on."

The girl looked at me quizzically, as though she had never considered me in that guise before in her life. My heart sank again. It must have been at my waistline by this point in proceedings.

Then a tear welled up in the corner of her right eye and I walked toward her with my arms outstretched. Despite her initial qualms, she fell into me and blubbered for several minutes. All the while, I concentrated on the aroma of her hair and the feel of her body under my palms.

"There, there." I patted her gently on the small of her back and waited for the sadness to abate. This was not how I envisaged the evening was going to progress.

When her sobbing ceased, Sylvia pushed us apart and fished out a compact from her clutch bag. Only now did I realize she was dressed to the nines and not wearing her usual set of A-line skirts and tight-fitting blouses. The black dress left nothing to the imagination. What an outfit to wear to dump someone.

I must admit I considered making a move on her there and then, but something stopped me just in time. Perhaps it was her doe-eyed expression or a single thread of common decency that had stubbornly remained inside me.

"Had you been together long?"

"Yes, six months, but I knew it was going nowhere. Whenever I mentioned getting more serious, Joe would change the subject."

"You can't trust men, Sylvia. Working here should have taught you that by now."

"You're right, Jake. Is there a reason you haven't settled down with anyone?"

"Most women don't like the hours I keep or the work that I do, which makes it hard to find that special someone."

"I know what you mean."

"Are you happy here, Sylvia?"

"I'd rather be in a bar, to be honest."

"That's not quite what I meant. Do you enjoy working at Adkins and Schwartz?"

"Oh yes, for certain."

"Let's get you that drink."

I picked up her coat and placed it over her shoulders. With a smile, she knocked back the rest of her Scotch and we left the building.

TUESDAY

8

THE NEXT MORNING, I paid a visit to Lou. And before you
wonder, I put Sylvia in a taxi the previous night and acted like a
perfect gentleman, more's the pity.

When I first popped over, he was out on a case and there was no
way to tell how long he'd be away from his desk. I figured there was
no harm waiting a while, so I went for a coffee along the block and
returned a half hour later. This time, he was back.

"Lou, you got five minutes?"

"For you, Jake, I'd take the whole day off."

I followed him into an interview room and he shut the door.

"What do you want, Jake?"

"I've spoken more with Mrs. Langchamp and now I understand
her better. I'm interested in your take on the dame."

"It hasn't changed since yesterday. A big lunk of a husband, they
argued, and he hit out at her. So she defended herself. What else is
there to say?"

"So you are telling me that the fact he was bigger than her was
enough for the DA not to bother to file charges?"

"That's the shape of it, Jake. You reckon she crept up on him
while he was unawares and attacked him before he knew what had
happened?"

"It is possible, Lou."

"Next time you go skulking over to Spencer, read the whole of his report and not just the summary page. There were no defensive wounds and not a solitary knife mark to his back or sides. They were all in his chest and stomach…"

"And the only way to get that pattern of blows was if she stood in front of him as she stabbed."

"Jake, despite what they say, you are smarter than you first appear."

"Appearances can be deceptive."

"Is your client fooling us?"

"That's what she's paying me to prove. Langchamp wants me to unearth evidence that your flatfeet can't find."

"Is there any to be found?"

"I'm not sure, Lou, to be honest. The neighbors are an interesting bunch. I wouldn't be surprised if there was a backstory which neither of us has got to the bottom of."

"My men found them to be the usual crop of nosey nobodies. Each couple was more concerned with scoring points over the others. Nothing to see there."

I stared across the squad room at the uniforms scurrying around the place, shifting paper from one desk to another. I was glad I'd never signed up, even though there was a moment in my young life when I had considered the prospect.

"Penny for your thoughts?"

"I'm happy I'm not out there."

Lou's gaze scanned the room, and he smiled.

"You'd have made a good cop."

"Maybe, but a lousy police officer. I don't enjoy wearing a uniform or being told what to do."

"I've noticed that about you, Jake."

"Fancy a coffee?"

Lou checked his watch and pulled a face.

"We can add a splash of something if that makes a difference?"

A nod and a smile and we sauntered out of the precinct house to a joint down the block, which we both knew well.

WE PROPPED UP the counter in O'Malley's bar and I ordered two coffees, one Irish for Lou.

"Tell me. Why do you believe that Mrs. Langchamp isn't a cold-blooded killer?"

Lou grinned at me.

"Jake, just because your client is paying you to make us poor cops appear stupid, doesn't mean I'm going to help you get the job done. Unless you're offering to share your wages?"

At face value, Lou sounded as if he was trying to take a bribe, but I knew him better than that.

"It's not the precinct that'll appear foolish, only your DA."

"Believe me, if the case ends up in court, I'll be the one to get it in the neck, even if the guy gets a conviction. So, before you run around telling everyone that your client did it and the dumb cops couldn't prove it, spare some consideration for me as I return to traffic duty."

"Aw, you know it's not like that, Lou. The case hasn't closed, so nobody looks foolish yet. If I unearth evidence next week, that's when the fertilizer hits the air conditioning."

Lou's eyes ground into my skull.

"But I'll be off the case by then. If I don't get the job resolved by this Friday, she stops paying me, and my interest in the death of Kole Langchamp withers on the vine."

He took a glug of his drink.

"All the evidence points to self-defense. Every minute she was in the precinct house, the woman was calm. And I mean cold as ice. Even when she thought she was on her own and we stared at her through the two-way mirror in the interview room."

"If you believe there's more to this, then why have you recommended to the district attorney not to pursue her?"

He was silent and tilted his head to one side for a second.

"Because you believe there is something hinky, and the DA thought otherwise."

"Jake, you could make a good detective one day."

"Have you not considered the possibility that she was in shock?"

"Yes, and dismissed it. You know how killers behave. If you had seen how calm she was, how quiet. Langchamp did not present herself as a woman who had been forced to murder her husband to save her own life. It was like she was at peace for the first time in a long while."

9

BACK AT THE Langchamp residence, I parked my jalopy two doors down and sat and waited. The trouble with surveillance is that it is boring work. You are stuck in a tiny space for hours on end with nothing to do but stare out the window. Your biggest fear is that if you turn away for more than a second, then you'll miss whoever it is you are hoping to catch.

If you are lucky, you are inside the tin can with someone to talk to, but more often you are forced to spend hours alone with only your thoughts for company. That's what did for Ed, my old partner. If I had been sitting next to him, perhaps he'd still be alive. Or we'd both be dead.

For once, I had the foresight to bring two packets of cigarettes with me, but I hadn't checked if I had enough matches. Three smokes in and I shoved my hands into every pocket in the hope I would find my lighter. It was lost in a fight over a year before, but somehow in my desperation, I thought I would discover it in my pants. No such luck.

Another hour ticked by and all I had to show for it was bupkis. Two men had walked up and down the street, each with a dog in tow. I had almost gone up to them to ask if they had a spare box of matches, but that is not what they teach you in private detective school. Stealth is the name of the game.

I considered balancing the time it would take me to pop to a store, buy a lighter, and return, but my fear of missing out prevented me from doing the sensible thing. There was a joint only a five-minute drive away, so I could have carried out the round trip in under fifteen. The temptation to turn the key over to start the engine was immense, but something held me back. I needed to hit the head and had forgotten to pack the usual bottle I reserved for such occasions.

This was going from bad to worse. I hopped out and scouted the area for a suitable hedge. No such luck, but on a neighboring street, I noticed a house with no lights on and open access to the backyard.

That was good enough for me, so I hurried round to the rear and relieved myself against a wall. It's not something I'm proud of, but needs must. Too much coffee and too few smokes make Jake a bad boy.

By the time I returned to my jalopy, a black sedan had appeared outside the Langchamp house. I slid behind the wheel and waited. Its lights winked off, and a man got out and strode to the front door. He was too far away, and it was too dark for me to see his face. Mrs. Langchamp smiled when she let him in with no conversation. Not only did she know him, but he was expected.

I waited for five minutes in case he had just dropped by to borrow a handsaw, but nobody surfaced. My car was the last place I needed to be right now, so I swung out and scurried round the back of the houses, only too aware that the nosey neighborhood gang would watch all the comings and goings with a keen eye. I did not want to be on their list.

By the time I reached the Langchamp backyard, two lights shone out of the first floor. One hailed from the kitchen and the other I had learned from the inside emanated from the through living room. I also knew that I'd be spotted if I just strolled across the yard, assuming anyone looked in my general direction so I couldn't take the chance.

I whisked along the edge of the lawn on the right-hand side, as far away from the living room window as I could. With my back flat to the house wall, I shimmied over until my head reached the kitchen window. I listened for any noise from within.

Nothing. I bent down and headed past the kitchen toward the living room. The curtains were still not drawn and I caught murmurings from inside. The two might not have been any more than six feet away from me, but the brickwork prevented me from knowing what they were up to, although I had a pretty good idea. I paused and waited, standing against the wall, my ears attempting to squeeze the life out of every sound I could discern.

AFTER AN ETERNITY, the wait almost killing me, I took a chance to bob my head forward a few inches, just enough to get a sense of what was happening inside. A man and a woman on a couch. That was all I saw, but that was sufficient for a first attempt. The good news was that I knew where they were, even if I could not identify them yet.

Now I could afford to be patient. It might have only been a split second, but they sat up close and personal. So that ruled out the guy being an insurance salesman making a late-night call. Or some brother or other family member I knew nothing about. This man seemed to be a friend, if you get my drift.

I bent down to take my head as low off the ground as possible and ruined a pair of pants by kneeling on the patio. That gave me a chance to pop my head out a little farther and a little longer. He held a tumbler containing less than half an inch of whiskey and she had a hand on his knee.

That was sufficient for my second viewing and, to be honest, there wasn't much more that I needed. Besides, Langchamp was entitled to ask a friend to visit, although you might have expected him to be comforting her rather than the other way round. Appearances can be deceptive, though, and I stuck around to discover what transpired.

I did nothing for several minutes because I reckoned the friend would take a while to finish his drink. Given Langchamp's impeccable tastes, I'd bet my bottom dollar that we were talking a single malt Scotch and not some cheap rubbish. The kind of liquor you savor and don't just throw down the back of your neck, no matter what life may offer you.

Either my ears were attuned to the situation or the guy dropped his glass onto the table, but I heard it land and a quick bob forwards delivered me the sight of the two walking out of the living room, hand in hand.

I flipped a coin in my head and it landed tails. So I searched around to find a tree and clambered up to the first branch as quietly as a man in a suit can. Clinging to the trunk, the foliage hid me so that when the bedroom light flipped on, you'd have to be eagle-eyed to spot me.

As Langchamp closed the drapes, the friend removed his pants. The guy had upgraded himself to something much more than a consoling, concerned acquaintance. Given what I knew would happen inside the house, I found no reason to stick around any longer. I'd seen two people rutting before and I felt no desire to repeat the experience, especially as the draperies were drawn.

I landed with an unfortunate thud back on the ground, but the couple had far more pressing matters to attend to rather than concern themselves about unusual sounds in the backyard. Within a few minutes, I sat in my car, considering my next move. I could wait here to find out when he left or go to my warm bed and get a good night's rest.

How important was it for me to know whether the guy was an aficionado of wham bam thank you mam or was prepared to stay the night? It made no difference to me. Langchamp entertained a man within a day of killing her husband. The headline wrote itself and nothing else mattered. My bed called me like a siren and I headed home via a drugstore. Damned if I was going to be without a light on another stakeout.

10

A NIGHT'S REST in my own bed was the best decision I ever made. And the worst. I hauled ass and got back to Avril's house, where the sedan remained where I had left it, thank goodness. On the way over, I hurtled by the trashmen heading toward the Langchamp's street.

Under ordinary circumstances, I would have waited for ages before the receptacles landed on the sidewalk or I'd be forced to hang out at the back of people's houses, hoping not to get caught. Why all the palaver? The contents of the trash become public property when it arrives on public land. Until then, the owner could sue me or, much worse, if she had a firearm at hand. And the person in question already had a track record of homicide.

So I had every right to go through the Langchamp's trash as it was on the sidewalk waiting for that morning's collection, but I did not have enough time to do a good job of it. My client or her lover might appear on the stoop any moment and there are few things as demeaning as being discovered by the person who's paying your wages elbow-deep in eggshells and spilled milk.

There was only one thing to do, and I wasn't happy about it. As disgusting as the contents might have been to search through, up close and personal, the trash had developed a stench like a science experiment gone horribly wrong. This was going to be an unpleasant job. I covered my mouth and nose with the handkerchief from the top pocket of my jacket to reduce the acrid aroma floating around the back of my throat and I got to work.

Some attempt at cooking had headed south if the appalling smell was anything to go by. Perhaps I had discovered the actual source of the Langchamp disagreement. He complained so much about her food that she threw it out. Later, she came at him for revenge? Maybe not.

Then I experienced a low rumble in my chest and my first instinct was that I was having a heart attack. I searched up and down the street for signs of an ambulance, but instead, there were the trashmen in the distance. No cardiac murmur after all, but a more present danger instead.

I have found that many government employees are helpful and hard-working, but every trashman I have met has taken an instant dislike to me rummaging around in their workplace. I don't blame them, but I never use physical violence except as a last resort. The same cannot be said of the knuckle scrapers who operate the trash van.

They were two blocks away and heading toward me, which meant I had a matter of minutes before I took a beating and lost any evidence that might be hidden in front of me.

More eggs, slivers of bacon rind, and a slice of toast with a solitary bite taken out of it. If I wanted to match dental records, then this was what I would need. But it wasn't what I required. I needed paperwork or some tangible explanation of why Langchamp did for Kole.

A quick glance up and the trash truck was only six houses away. The guys hadn't seen me yet, but it was only a matter of time now. I swallowed hard, and in my anxiety, I fell backward and landed flat on the ground. Picking myself up, I didn't waste valuable seconds dusting myself down.

I resumed my squatting position and continued my work. For every moment I stared into the metal abyss, I'd glance down the street to gauge how long I had left. I wanted to avoid a beating.

Despite the disgusting mess before me, I did my best to pick through the interesting items and leave the dregs of Satan behind. Papers, newsprint, anything that would tell me something more about Mrs. Langchamp, her husband, and their life together. I have an unhealthy interest in scrunched balls of paper because that indicates a person's emotional state when they threw it into the trash. A calm individual folds the page once, but to destroy the flatness of the item often is an indicator of a need to hide the contents from prying eyes. And that was my stock-in-trade.

THE FIRST THING was to pile up any papers I could get my hands on. The older ones were at the bottom, of course, and they were of most interest because they would have been discarded days before Kole's death. But did I mention how many eggs were skulking around in that metal tin?

I shoved my arm as far as I could reach and found what I was hoping would be the mother lode: a ball of paper. I chucked it onto the ground and slammed my foot on top of it to stop it from rolling away. Apart from that, there were slim pickings. A utility bill, several letters addressed to the occupier, nothing interesting.

Yet another glance up and the trashmen were next door. As they took the neighbor's trash from the sidewalk to their truck and back, they eyed me up and muttered to each other. It was time to do what every hero must: run away like a yellow-streaked coward. I grabbed my bundle of dirty papers and hightailed it to the rear of the house, careful to avoid walking past any windows in case Langchamp had managed to ease her way out of her bed.

The clattering noise from the kitchen told me I had made the right decision, and I clung to the brickwork like gum to a shoe. Pinned to the rear wall of the house, I peeked around the corner as the trash van trundled over to the next set of houses.

Of course, this meant I was free to escape in a minute, but there was now open ground between me and the sidewalk. Any of Langchamp's illustrious neighbors could spot me and report to her what I was up to.

The only reason I went garbage diving in the first place was that I didn't believe Langchamp would consent to me checking out her trash, otherwise, I wouldn't have put myself through all that. As much as I trusted her motives for wanting to be proven guilty, in the pit of my stomach, something didn't smell right in the kingdom of Denmark. Although, that could just have been my hands, which had spent more time in that trashcan than was appropriate in the life of one human being.

I took a breath and decided what to do next. The ball of paper was burning a hole in my curiosity.

Still squatting, I unraveled the scrunched-up communication. The outside surface of the wrinkled sheet might have been sticky, but what was written was gold. How often do you get to read a death threat aimed at a murder victim? For me, it was the first and last time in my entire sleuthing career.

Dear Mrs. Langchamp

You don't know me, but I know you. This letter is to make you aware that if necessary, I will see that Kole dies so that my brother can find happiness with you like he was always meant to.

I know what you've been doing, and it needs to stop immediately. Elmo deserves his chance and your actions are preventing him from living in El Dorado.

Franny Kennard

Questions bounced around my head like it was a pinball machine, but there was no time to ponder anything, because no sooner had I finished reading the epistle than the front door rattled open and I flung myself on the ground under the kitchen window.

Hindsight tells me that this was unnecessary as the action happened facing the street, but my instincts for self-preservation were strong. I rolled over and peeked around the corner again. Nothing. I still didn't want the neighbors to tell tales about me, so I remained where I was and my ears strained to catch every noise that emanated from the house.

Footsteps… and my heart almost leaped out of my mouth. A car engine spluttered into life and I figured the houseguest was leaving. I waited until the sound of the vehicle had faded and ran for my car to give chase.

11

FOR A CHASE to happen, we need two things. Someone to know they are being followed and somebody else doing the following. And what we had here only involved me catching up with the guy and tailing him until he reached his destination.

After all, he was behaving like an ordinary joe who'd spent the night with his woman. He wasn't gunning the engine and speeding off down the road to evade capture. His casual journey showed a man pleased with himself and how the evening had turned out.

A fifteen-minute drive later and the car stopped in front of a residential block. The guy entered the building, but I couldn't get to the entrance in time to find out which apartment he was visiting.

Instead, I scanned the names next to the buzzers and one stood out from all the rest: E Kennard. Now, I may not have been first in line when they handed out brains, but I was prepared to put money down that this was the residence of Elmo, brother of Franny and somebody whose happiness was linked to the life of Mrs. A.J. Langchamp and her deceased husband, Kole.

I had done enough skulking around for one day and it wasn't even close to lunchtime, so I figured that I'd take the direct approach and pressed the buzzer. Without being asked to identify myself, Elmo buzzed me in and I used the elevator to reach the third floor. Left down the corridor and second on the right.

Before I got a chance to knock on the door, it opened and there stood the man I'd witnessed in Langchamp's bedroom last night.

"Can I help?"

I flashed my PI badge and asked to come in. No doubt mistaking me for a cop, he smiled and led me into a kitchen diner. No wonder they'd met at hers; in this place, you'd smash your knuckles on the walls every time you stretched. Either Elmo wasn't flush with green or he was one of those miser millionaires. A glance at the quality of the furniture showed it was the former. A threadbare couch and an old armchair screamed out thrift store.

"I am investigating the murder of Kole Langchamp."

"You can't think that I had anything to do with it."

"Did you?"

"Not at all. I remained here all Sunday night."

"How can you be so sure you were here then?"

"I'm always in. I don't lead what most would describe as an exciting life."

"Apart from yesterday evening."

His cheeks heated up. He opened his mouth and closed it again, unsure what to say.

"Let me save you the bother of trying to work out a better answer, Elmo. You spent last night with AJ and the night before her husband was killed. Did you sleep at your place or with her after he died?"

"At home. I'm a close friend and I popped over to console her, what with Kole being dead and all."

"All night long?"

I couldn't stop the smirk spreading across my face, and Elmo's cheeks got even hotter.

"Don't worry about it, Elmo. What you get up to with your closest pals is none of my business. All I'm trying to find out is how Kole died."

"Didn't she confess to the police, Mr.?"

"Adkins, but my friends call me Jake. And yes, she admitted to the killing."

"Well, Jake. There you have it."

"Not really. I said I wanted to know how Mr. Langchamp died, not who claimed they'd murdered him."

He fell into silence for a spell, thinking through the distinction I had drawn.

"Are you a cop?"

"Private detective. I've been hired to investigate the homicide."

"AJ mentioned she'd hired you. She phoned me as soon as the deed was done."

"How do you know she rang so quickly afterward?"

"She told me so, and I'll swear on any Bible in this land that she was distraught when she called."

"Did you notice when this happened?"

"Nope, but you tell me what time the murder occurred and I will testify that she phoned me five minutes later."

ELMO WANTED TO please more than he wanted anyone to know the truth. His loyalty to AJ was touching but annoying, at least for me. The best thing to do was leave and grab a bite to eat. In all the excitement, I'd forgotten to down any breakfast and I must have been the fella who invented brunch because I chowed down on toast and scrambled egg in a diner on my way to the office.

As I swallowed the dregs of my coffee, I realized there was another tack to take with Elmo, so I paid the check and scooted back to the apartment block. A quick press of his buzzer and nothing. Peculiar. Another stab at the button but still nada.

I waited by the entrance until a woman exited ten minutes later. As ever, I pretended to peruse the buzzers and as soon as she walked out, I popped my foot out to prevent the closing door from locking and entered the lobby.

Up to the third floor and over to Elmo's apartment. I formed a fist to knock on the door, but it was already ajar.

"Elmo?"

No response. I pulled out my piece from its holster under my jacket and stepped inside, nice and slow. In these situations, either you're going to find zip or someone is aiming their gun at you. The cautious man lives to enjoy another day.

With my revolver in front of me, I peeked round the corner to check out the living room. Empty. Next, I sidled over to the kitchen. Again, nothing. Then through the only other door to a bedroom and shower. Both were as devoid of people as the rest of the place.

But the bedroom should have been declared a disaster area. Every single drawer had been pulled out, and the contents thrown on the floor. The sole wardrobe was open, with a pile of clothes strewn nearby. I had no idea what was being searched for or whether the quarry had been found.

I holstered my piece and sat on the end of the bed. Had Elmo rifled through his own belongings to find who-knows-what, or was this an abduction scene? There was only one way for me to find out.

A CIVILIAN WOULD have called the cops; I knew that, but the last thing I needed was a conversation with Lou about how I should leave police business to government employees. I wasn't in the humor for it. Instead, I hopped downstairs in search of the super. They know everything about the occupant of every room in their building. I figure it's why they take the job in the first place.

"Have you seen Elmo Kennard today?"

"Not so's I recall."

The man hunched before me did not come across like your typical building supervisor. Most of them can stand up straight and are handy with a hammer. This one appeared as though the only thing he did well was to sweat heavily.

"How about over the weekend?"

A pause. The chump took my question seriously.

"Nope, can't say I did."

"When did you see him last? Can you remember?"

Another silence as he stared at his shoes. I hoped he was doing me a favor and thinking. At this point, narcolepsy was a distinct possibility.

"Not for a while. I try not to get involved in the lives of the residents, you know? First, you ask how they are of a morning. The next minute, they're telling you their life story and asking you to fix their plumbing."

Times were tough in the building management business and this doofus was proving less useful than a chocolate coffee pot.

"Did you hear any commotion this morning or notice anyone unusual around these parts?"

"Apart from you?

"Excluding me."

A long surveillance of his toecaps ensued. He looked up at me with a smile on his face and I discerned a glimmer in the corner of his eyes that some insight had just flashed through his mind.

"No, sir."

I thanked him for his time out of politeness and walked back to the entranceway. Judging by the signage, which proved more helpful than an hour with the super, the building housed a basement parking lot, so I ambled down the stairwell in search of Elmo's vehicle.

Sure enough, in the bay allocated to his apartment number, I found his black sedan. I checked the license plate, and it was his, all right. I tried the door handles, but they were locked. Then took a quick glance across the sea of vehicles to check whether I had company. Nobody.

Just before I set about jimmying the trunk using the contents of Old Faithful, stiletto heels rang around the lot and a woman walked toward me. She must have taken the stairs from the entrance hall.

"I think I saw you earlier on. Weren't you talking with Elmo?"

"Yes, and you are...?"

"Ursula Varley. I live opposite him."

I flashed my badge in response and wondered why she had sought me out and how she had found me in the basement of her building.

12

"DID YOU HEAR anything unusual this morning?"

"Apart from you rattling around Elmo's place a few minutes ago?"

"Yes, Miss Varley."

"Oh, use my first name, Ursula. Whenever someone calls me Miss Varley, I look round to find where my mother is."

I smiled.

"I'm Adkins, but my friends call me Jake."

"Well, Mr. Adkins." I winced. "There were voices raised an hour earlier."

"Could you make out what was said, Ursula?"

"No, Jake. It's not like I'm a person who'd press her ear to the door to get a better listen."

"Was Elmo's door shut too?"

She beamed, then crossed her arms. I must have hit the nail on the head.

"Could you tell if Elmo was talking with a man or a woman?"

"Not really. Everything was so muffled."

I eyed her from top to bottom and wondered why this beautiful girl glued her ear to her front door to eavesdrop on her neighbor. Then it hit me.

"Were you friends with Elmo?"

"We were neighbors, Jake. That much is obvious."

"Sure, but were you more than people who lived in the same corridor as each other, Ursula?"

She bit her lip.

"That is a most impertinent question to ask a young lady."

"I'm afraid it's part of my job. I make inquiries about the darker side of life."

"What we had together wasn't dark."

Now it was my turn to smile. My hunch was right. Elmo was entertaining two women at the same time. What a player.

"So, you are fond of him?"

"Yes, he's a lot of fun to be around."

"I'm sure he is. The sort of guy who's always willing to please."

She frowned, then her face relaxed into a slack expression.

"We were supposed to go out this afternoon, but I doubt if that is going to happen now."

"If you don't mind me asking, how do you afford your apartment?"

"I'm a typist."

"So, shouldn't you be at work and not planning assignations with Elmo?"

"I phoned in sick this morning."

She placed her palm on her belly to mime the alleged cause of her illness.

"And your office accepted your story?"

"Let's just say that my boss and I have an understanding."

She didn't need to wink at me, because I knew what she meant, but she chose to anyway. Feisty.

"Perhaps we might continue our conversation in your apartment? That way we'd be more comfortable and perhaps you could offer me a cup of java."

"Jake, that's very forward of you."

"No disrespect intended, Ursula. I just thought you'd rather experience the comforts of your home than the smell of oil and gas fumes for company."

She toyed with her necklace for a second, considering my proposal. A car screeched past, taking a corner a little too fast, and that decided for her.

"My place will be more pleasant."

She rotated on one foot and glided back on the route she'd come. I followed her, enjoying the way her ass wiggled as she propelled herself forward. I'm not surprised Elmo wanted more than just to borrow a cup of sugar.

THE ELEVATOR APPEARED palatial when I rode up the first time, but somehow Ursula and I were packed like sardines. We stood only a few inches apart, facing each other as we headed up to the third. Perhaps it was my imagination or was she puffing her chest out at me? The bell dinged to tell us we had arrived at our destination, and she led the way down the corridor.

Her hallway and Elmo's were identical, but as soon as we entered the living room, you knew this was a bigger apartment.

"Two bedrooms?"

"Uh-huh."

"This must have cost a pretty penny."

"Hank was kind enough to help me out."

"Who's he?"

"My boss."

Elmo might have been a player, but Ursula was a complete team. I always admire anybody who can work an angle and she was one such cookie. And she worked her charms on everyone, including me.

I walked over to the window and peeped out. She had an excellent view of the entire frontage, although the apartment was right on top of the entranceway itself.

"You get to spot everyone's comings and goings from here."

"If I wanted to, Jake. But I don't spend my life watching others from the sidelines. I want to grab every experience with both hands, you know?"

I understood. This woman in her early twenties was making the most of everything she had. I might have caught her eavesdropping on her lover, but she had a string of men in tow and wasn't the least bit ashamed of using them for her own ends: like Hank's contribution to her rent here.

"Did Elmo help you out? Buying you things, and so on?"

"He's been kind enough to give me some gifts."

She placed her fingers on her pearl necklace again.

"Do you drive?"

"Oh, I see what you mean. Yes, he bought me my car."

Ursula was transactional to the end. Buy her something and she'll put out. Come across like you'll spend hundreds and the woman will show you her living room. And here I was standing in the very place.

"Is that coffee still on offer?"

"Ooh, where are my manners? Sit down, Jake, and I'll make up a fresh batch."

I settled into one of the leather couches. The pair must have cost more than a month's wages. Perhaps she had been helped by Hank or Elmo. Or maybe a third man she hadn't told me about yet.

Ursula carried in a tray with a coffee pot, two mugs, a milk jug, a bowl of sugar, and a plate of cookies. She knew the way to a man's heart and his stomach was no doubt her second favorite organ. She fussed over the drinks until we both relaxed into the same couch, our knees almost touching.

"Mighty fine. Thank you."

"You're welcome, Jake."

We remained silent for a few seconds. As much as I wanted to find out more about this woman, I wasn't sure she had more to offer my case.

"What kind of car did he buy you?"

"I know nothing about marques. It's black. A sedan."

"Is it downstairs in the lot now?"

"No, Elmo borrows it on account of me not having a reserved space at work. He brings it back at the weekend for me to use and he has it during the week."

The guy was a smart man. Her name is on the pink slip and he gets to run around town to be with AJ, except on weekends.

"But he parked it in his allocated spot and not yours?"

"It's an easier space to drive into."

I couldn't argue with that. As she leaned forward to pick up her cup, her hand brushed against my knee. We both stared at my leg, glanced at each other, and she brought the mug to her lips and pouted a little before taking a sip.

"Would you like a tour around the rest of the apartment?"

"Don't mind if I do."

We popped our heads around the kitchen door. It was well-appointed, filled with shiny gadgets. Tidy. Then we pootled through the living room and down a corridor that Elmo's place didn't have. Three doors were before us. She tapped on the nearest. "Guest bathroom."

I nodded because I had no desire to check out the john and she had no interest in showing me. The next door along got opened. "Second bedroom," was the only description she provided me.

"You could be a real estate agent."

A playful grin ripped across her face.

"And here we have the master bedroom and en suite bathroom."

I stood and stared. The theme of the room was white lace, and everything seemed just perfect, but expensive. One kink in the armor was the ceiling mirror right above the bed: the minx.

There was no place to sit other than on her bed; it didn't seem appropriate for me to use her dressing table chair. Ursula sat next to me and picked a piece of fluff from my shoulder that was too small for me to spot. Judging by the sparkle in her eyes and the way she licked her lips, this was going to be an enjoyable interrogation.

"Have you ever heard a woman's voice in Elmo's apartment?"

"Why yes, of course."

"How so?"

"His sister visits from time to time."

"Franny?"

"Uh-huh."

She ran a finger down my jacket lapel and rested on the bulge.

"Is that a gun?"

"Yep."

She swallowed hard.

"Ursula, I was talking about any other woman that Elmo might have as a visitor."

"Whatever do you mean?"

"Does he have any other female friends?"

Her fingertip was just about to weave its way under my shirt between two buttons over my chest. Then she yanked it away and stood up.

"You'd better go now, Mr. Adkins."

"So he has had no other women in his apartment?"

"Get out."

I took her tone to indicate the answer was yes and hustled into the corridor as I was no longer welcome.

13

URSULA MIGHT HAVE been a vixen, but she was of no substantive use to me. She'd heard nothing. She had seen less. All I had discovered was that she had a fiery temper if you suggested that the men she slept with were prepared to sleep with other women too.

But the letter I had rescued from the trash was something else. Franny Kennard threatened Kole's life. Did that mean that AJ was protecting her? Had they conspired over his downfall? Was the sister just a crazy person who spoke volumes but did nothing?

I knew none of the answers and figured the best plan was to extract as much information from the police as I could. After all, they wouldn't throw me out of their bedroom if I hit on a raw nerve.

Lou refused to see me when I arrived at the front desk of the precinct. I told the sergeant that I'd wait for a more convenient time.

"It's your funeral, Mac."

Ten minutes later, Inspector Granger appeared and walked straight past me. I followed him to O'Malley's and bought us both Irish coffees. We clinked mugs and sipped at our drinks.

"To what do I owe this pleasure, Jake?"

"I've been digging around and unearthed two people of interest."

"Oh?"

A twitch in the corner of his mouth told me he was stringing me along. It was the same tell he had when he played poker.

"A brother and sister act, Elmo and Franny Kennard."

"What about them?"

I sighed.

"When were you going to mention them, Lou?"

"Now... since you've asked about the pair."

"Lou, why do you make my life so difficult?"

"You're the one getting the big bucks. I figured the least you should do is earn it, like the rest of us working stiffs."

He had a point.

"Do you know where Elmo was the night of the murder?"

"That I do, Jake."

I glared at my old friend, who was proving less helpful than Ursula, only she was a damn sight more attractive.

"Spill, Lou."

He glanced at me and smirked.

"He has a perfect alibi for the night in question. Elmo was with his sister that evening."

"You interviewed both of them?"

"Just him, who told us he was with Franny."

"How did you find out about him so quickly?"

"That would let you in on the secrets of a police detective."

"I know. Tell me and stop messing around."

"We found an item of clothing in the back of Mrs. Langchamp's drawers with his initials on. We asked her what it was all about and she told us."

"With those topflight detecting skills, I'm surprised you haven't made it to captain by now."

"Can't stand the paperwork and wouldn't want to be stuck in an office all on my own, away from the clatter of the department."

"That'd be the death of all hope for a chump like you."

Silence descended as we consumed our coffees.

"Does that mean you haven't interviewed the sister?"

"Correct."

"So, how can you be sure that Elmo's alibi holds water?"

"Why would he lie?"

"You're kidding me, right? To hide the fact that he killed Kole and AJ is taking the rap."

"Jake, the best you've got is that Mrs. Langchamp admits to murdering her husband to save her lover and risks fifteen to life to do so."

Hearing the idea spoken out loud made me rethink the proposition.

"Now that you say it like that."

"And that's why I believed him when he said he was with his sister."

I shuffled in my seat and sipped at my drink.

"What if I told you that Franny had threatened Kole's life less than a week before the guy was killed?"

"I'd say that it is less believable that Mrs. Langchamp would take the fall to protect the sister of her lover. What benefit is there for her? Besides, there's no evidence to suggest that there was anybody in the house on the night of the murder apart from the married couple."

"Yeah…"

"Anyway, aren't you supposed to be finding a way to prove your client guilty and not to pin the blame on a third party?"

He was right. The more I investigated the death of Kole Langchamp, the greater the number of other suspects I was uncovering. That wasn't my job.

"This case is getting too complicated for me, Lou."

"It's what you've been paid to do."

I flicked a glance at the inspector.

"How do you know the terms of my contract?"

"I've met you before, Jake. You always ask for payment up front. When was the last time you chased a client for money?"

"Yes, there is that, but it doesn't make the situation any less messy."

"The DA is happy to leave this baby alone and count it as voluntary manslaughter."

"From everything I've heard and seen, it was a crime of passion. I don't believe AJ intended to kill Kole that night, but she wants her day in court, so the world knows that's the situation. A lady like her doesn't want her name tainted with any suggestion of impropriety."

"Slaying her spouse isn't improper?"

"Do not play word games with me, Lou. You know what I mean."

"Sure, but we have the confession of a woman with no priors and no reason to lie. Her husband was a gorilla, and he drove her to the edge. There hasn't been a more open-and-shut case since I joined law enforcement. Why should the district attorney waste public money on a trial that he has no appetite to put on? And every jury in the state will take one look at the grieving widow and send her home with a tear running down their collective cheeks."

"I need more time to figure this out."

"You want more time, but the DA has been very clear. The case must stop gathering dust on his desk by the end of business this Friday. Either we charge her with something other than voluntary manslaughter or we wave goodbye and leave the woman to build a new life in the wake of her husband's untimely departure at her hands."

"What if I told you I could prove that someone else had done the deed?"

"Who would that be, Jake?"

"I'd rather not say, for now, until a get a stronger line, but there is something I have found that your cops on the scene missed."

"If you have any hard evidence putting someone other than Mrs. Langchamp holding the knife, then you know you must hand it over to me. Obstruction of justice will place you inside a cell and I won't be able to protect you. Not this time."

I gulped. An overnight stint in a precinct jail is one thing, but a month in the Lincoln Heights facility two Christmases ago was more than I ever needed to learn not to break the law and be caught.

My refusal to hand over evidence and my manner in court led the judge to throw me behind bars, but Lou knew I would not reveal my source. He got me out by persuading the then DA to convince the judge that I was not in contempt, just stupid. He pushed on an open door and I was released for New Year's Eve.

"The end of Friday or first thing Monday can't make any difference to the district attorney, but it might be enough time for me to get my client indicted."

"Will you listen to yourself for a moment? What kind of cockamamie PI are you? You'll be laughed out of the private eye guild if you keep jabbering away like that."

He was right, and my words were absurd.

"So the end of next week is out of the question?"

Lou chuckled and ordered us a couple of shots to add to our laden coffees.

"You think I'm wasting my time, don't you?"

"Jake, a dame is paying you to prove her guilty of murder when she plainly is not. How she spends her money is up to her and what you do to earn your daily bread is between you, your accountant, and the IRS."

"The holy trinity."

We crossed ourselves and finished the remains of our drinks. The back of my throat burned because of the cheap Scotch the bartender had used. This was a cops' drinking den, after all.

"One last thing, Lou. Are there any other suspects you've spoken to, but not mentioned to me until now?"

"Finally, you're asking me some smart questions."

"And?"

"You know what I know. There's nothing else I've held back."

We shook hands and parted ways.

14

IF LOU HAD given up all that he knew, then that meant I needed to start back at square one, with the scene of the crime. Why would AJ have planned to murder Kole? Perhaps she threw out Franny's letter because it was ridiculous and not because the sister had anything on my client.

I grabbed some food-to-go from a local diner near my office and headed back to South Fifth Plaza and the Langchamp residence. I doubted whether AJ would appreciate me dropping crumbs on her floorboards, so I stayed in my vehicle while I chomped through my roast beef and tomato on rye.

As I finished the first half of my meal, a taxi arrived and halted outside AJ's. She appeared a minute later and hopped into the rear. I stared at my sandwich and considered tailing her, but the chances were that she'd be off to buy some groceries and not much else. Besides, I had told myself to go back to the scene of the crime, and that's precisely where I was.

Remaining in my car, I licked my fingers and motored through the rest of my food. Then I consumed my coffee and considered my next move. Breaking and entering always has an appeal, but I'd spent too much time in this neighborhood hoping not to get caught.

It was a worse feeling than being a kid in the candy shop while my mom and the store owner were deep in conversation about someone on the street who died of old age. I wanted to put my hand in that jar, but I knew that if I was spotted, there'd be hell to pay.

The neighbors here were like hawks. I'd been lucky so far, but only a terrible gambler assumes their winning streak will last forever. The trick is to play a long game, so I remained in the car, slumped down in the seat to make it harder for anyone to notice me in the vehicle, and waited.

Thirty tedious minutes later and I was greeted with the sight of a hobo rummaging through the street's trash. He wasn't the brightest because even I knew that the trashmen had been down the street earlier that day. But that didn't stop this bum from investigating the day's spoils. I sighed and when he paused at AJ's trashcan, I walked over to have a word.

AS I SAUNTERED toward the guy, he straightened up and walked away, but I caught up in a couple of paces.

"Hey, you. Do you mind if I ask you a few questions?"

A flash of my badge and he stopped in his tracks.

"Whatever they say, I wasn't there, and I done nothing."

"Nobody has accused you of anything. You're not in any trouble."

I smiled at him to offer some reassurance, but I'm not sure it did any good.

"I ain't done nothing. And you cops can't prove otherwise."

"Like I said, I only want to take up a few minutes of your time to find out some stuff."

"You want my time, do you?"

He paused for a moment and stared at the cigarette hanging from the corner of my mouth.

"Well, that'll cost you."

I offered him a smoke and lit it for him. "Much obliged."

He inhaled deeply and closed his eyes for a second as he let the flavor of my cheap brand roam around what was left of his palette. He was in heaven.

"You were working your way through the trash."

"Ain't no law against that. They're on the sidewalk. I know my rights."

"I'd checked them out myself earlier today before the trashmen came collecting."

"Oh, really."

He raised himself to his full height, and I realized he was taller than me.

"Find any tasty tidbits, fella?"

"They sure throw out a lot of food around here, don't they?"

"You betcha. That's why I work these streets so often. You can guarantee a complete breakfast and dinner from these two blocks."

"These people discard entire meals?"

"No, stupid. But you pick out enough fine morsels from the trashcans along this street alone to make yourself a three-courser, if you're that way inclined. Me? I am happy with a burger, fries, and a soda."

"From three separate trash cans?"

"That's what I'm telling you."

The bum tutted at me, as though he couldn't understand why I was so slow on the uptake.

"Have you ever found anything interesting in that trashcan?"

"That was a mighty fine cigarette, mister. You know what goes well with a smoke?"

"What's that?"

"A hot cup of coffee."

I smiled. The guy might live on the streets, but he was smarter than most.

"Would a mug of java help you answer my questions?"

"I reckon so."

A glint in his eye showed he was warming to me. I took him one block north and two east until we reached a diner I'd passed every time I visited AJ's house. Before we entered the premises, I slapped his coat three or four times to knock some of the dust and dirt off it. Then I tidied up his collar.

WE WALKED IN and if there had been a piano in the room, then it would have stopped playing, but I paid no attention and found us a booth. A waitress arrived within seconds.

"Would you gentlemen prefer somewhere quieter near the back?"

"No, we're good here, thank you. Can we have two coffees, please?"

As I spoke, she stared at the bum opposite me.

"Would you care to see the menu?"

The guy glanced at me and then he returned to staring at our server.

"Nothing for me, but perhaps my friend might like something. A piece of pie, maybe?"

He shook his head.

"No, make that a burger and fries."

A big grin spread across his face. The waitress gritted her teeth and hurried away.

"I never asked your name."

"No, you didn't. You want to know it?"

I nodded.

"People call me Pete."

"And is that your name?"

He guffawed, louder than our server would have liked.

"Good one, fella."

"Call me Jake."

"Were you really dumpster diving this morning, Jake?"

"Yessir."

"Did you find any tasty tidbits?"

"You might say that, Pete."

"Dang. No offense, but I wish I'd got there before you. Despite what I said earlier, there's been slim pickings these last few weeks."

"Why do you keep coming back?"

"Life is cyclical. Some times are good, others bad, but that pattern always repeats itself."

"And nothing special about the trash you were looking in when I caught up with you earlier?"

The waitress arrived with our drinks and delivered cream and sugar too. Pete added enough cubes to sink the Titanic.

"Well, two nights ago, the contents were of note."

"How so?"

Our server interrupted again to provide Pete with his burger. His eyes popped out of his skull when the plate arrived before him and I swear he salivated in front of me. Then he closed his eyes for a second. Was that a prayer? And tucked in.

"Tastes good."

"What was interesting, Pete?"

"Huh?"

"You said the trashcan had something you weren't expecting."

"Did I?"

"Hey, Pete. Don't do this to me."

Perhaps he detected the note of despair in my voice, but he chuckled again.

"Just messing with you. Mighty fine patty, by the way."

"And…?"

"There was an entire meal. Two, now that I think about it more."

"What?"

"You heard me right. Still on the plates."

"What did you do?"

"Ate me one for breakfast and saved the other for later, of course. What the hell do you reckon I'd do with them?"

He had a point; it was a dumb question and I should have known better.

The waitress had given up trying to hustle us out, and the other patrons weren't as concerned about our existence as she had feared. She refilled our coffees and left us alone again.

"Pete, was there anything else you might have noticed in the trash that day?"

"The plates sat on a bed of paper."

"What's that?"

"You ain't good at hearing, are you? I said there were piles of papers under the plates."

"Handwritten letters? That kind of thing?"

"No, Jake. These were typed with fancy letterheads."

"Did you read any of them?"

"I was looking for food, not searching for documentation."

"When I searched through the same trashcan the following day, there was nothing like you described in there."

"Of course not. I took them out and used them later."

"You just told me you didn't read them."

"I didn't; burned them to keep myself warm."

I slapped my forehead in frustration, but there was nothing I could do now. What might have been the key to this case was up in smoke before AJ had been released from the precinct house.

The waitress came over to clear the plates and top up Pete's mug. I asked for the check and he gave me the most pitiful doe-eyes.

"A piece of pie for my friend, please."

He grinned again.

"Listen, Jake. You're an upright fella. Most people won't give me the time of day, let alone spring for a meal in a warm diner."

"You've been very helpful, Pete. We've all got to look after one another."

I paid the check and left two five-dollar bills for a tip so that Pete could stay as long as he liked before heading back out into the world.

"Here's something for your time, Pete."

I slipped him a twenty as we shook hands and he gawped in wonder at the green.

"Don't mention it, Jake. Be sure to say hello when you're in this part of town again."

As I sauntered out, I glanced back and watched him palm half of the waitress's tip. Then he shrugged and took the other half before hightailing it out of the other entrance.

15

YOU'D IMAGINE THERE'D only be one person with a name like Franny Kennard in Los Angeles, but I can report that there are three in the phone book. The first two didn't have any brothers, let alone any called Elmo, which meant my last trip to Franny Kennard was certain to be the person that I wanted.

I knocked on her apartment door in a building on West Palm Street and South Oleander Avenue. She had darting eyes and mousy hair, which needed a brush.

"I'm Jake Adkins and I'm investigating the death of Kole Langchamp."

The woman before me froze for an instant.

"You'd better come in, Mr. Adkins."

"Call me Jake, all my friends do."

A half smile and she opened the door to give me space to enter. I perched in an armchair and Franny hovered on the edge of her floral-print couch. I glanced around the place and bright colors shone everywhere. Vibrant shades filled the living room, but no two seemed to match.

"Feel free to smoke if you like."

I took her up on her kind offer and lit a cigarette. She scuttled over to a drawer in her sideboard and rested an ashtray next to me on a small table.

"I figured someone would show up, eventually."

"Why's that Miss Kennard?"

"Because of all the goings on at the Langchamp house."

"What sort of thing do you mean?"

"You must know if you are carrying out an investigation."

"It would help if you could be more specific. Was there anything happening of note in Kole and Avril Langchamp's home?"

"I wouldn't want to say."

She kept her cards close to her ample chest. Why let me in if she had nothing useful to tell me? I tried a different angle.

"Did you feel any animosity toward Kole?"

"There's no need to be like that. Just because the man's dead doesn't give you the right to make bold accusations against a person."

"My apologies if you are offended by my question. Perhaps instead, you'd explain why somebody spotted you around the Langchamp residence on the night of the murder."

Her jaw dropped.

"Someone saw me?"

"Uh-huh. So there's no need to deny it."

"How did they know it was me and not some other woman?"

"Miss Kennard, you've told me it was you, so don't be so defensive. I'm only interested in the reason you skulked around in the bushes outside the house."

She sighed and ran her fingers through her hair.

"I wanted to see if Elmo was with that woman."

"Had they been seeing each other for a long time?"

"Weeks, not months, but they had become an item."

"Despite Mrs. Langchamp's marriage to her husband."

"If you're going to judge, you should leave right now. Affairs of the heart are unfathomable."

I stubbed out my smoke and wondered what a guy had to do around here to be offered a cup of java.

"DO YOU HAVE a coffee?"

"Yes, of course."

I waited a short while until Franny reappeared with our drinks. I considered following her into the kitchen, but I reckoned she was more comfortable with me not hovering over her. She returned with two mugs.

"Tastes good. Thank you."

A smile. "You're welcome, Jake."

"So tell me what brought you around to South Fifth Plaza."

"I wanted to see AJ for myself. After all, I'd heard about her from Elmo."

"What kinds of things had he told you?"

"How he enjoyed being with her. That she was smart and funny and knew how to get people to do her bidding. Men especially."

"She certainly has a way with her."

"And I figured she was a bad influence on him."

"What do you mean?"

"They were up to something, but I never found out what."

"AJ and Kole?"

"Langchamp and my brother, of course."

"They were sleeping with each other, right?"

"I don't know. Were they?"

I shook my head, confused. What was Franny talking about if it wasn't AJ's infidelity?

"What on earth…?"

"They were involved in some deal. Elmo hasn't given me any details, but he's expecting to get a lot of money out of it."

"Was Kole mixed up in it too?"

"I have no idea."

"But what about the letter you sent AJ?"

"You read it?"

"In a manner of speaking, yes. You sounded like you were threatening Kole's life. You talked about killing him."

"Oh no, not at all. I was being poetic. I yearned to destroy his soul so that AJ focused on him and didn't embroil him in her web of deceit."

"And what did you mean when you said to AJ that Elmo could only be happy if Kole was dead?"

"You're mixed up, Jake. I wanted him to be free from AJ and whatever financial scheme they were creating. He'll never find true happiness if the money he earns is based on deception and lies."

I sipped my coffee and sniffed the air for the smell of reefer. Either she'd had a puff before I arrived or she'd lost her mind. Whichever it was, Franny made little sense.

But if AJ and Elmo were scamming somebody, that might explain why she wanted to plead guilty to murder just to take the cops' attention away from her fraudulent activities.

"Do you know who the mark was?"

"What?"

"If they were carrying out a scam, then there must be someone they are tricking. Who's that?"

"No idea."

"So what makes you believe there were committing fraud?"

"The way Elmo talked about what the two of them were up to. He admitted spending time with her, but insisted that her marriage wasn't in jeopardy because of what they were doing."

"Have you considered the possibility that they were just good friends?"

Franny snorted.

"Not really. I mean, of course at first, but they spent every day together and Elmo refused to tell me where they went. The man had something to hide."

"And how do you know that money was involved?"

"Over the last week, especially, my brother has been telling me he's about to make a big score. There isn't anyone else who occupies his time. So it must be that he and AJ are cooking something up."

"But you have no evidence of this? It's just supposition."

"Jake, I might not have a confession from him of what he's done, but there isn't any other sensible explanation, is there?"

"And you know they are only friends because Elmo has told you."

"Right."

"Franny, have you ever asked if he is spending time under the sheets with AJ?"

"How dare you? Don't talk to people like that."

Franny's shock at my language belied what was going on in her head. She must have imagined much worse to shift her attention away from the bedroom and onto the boardroom. Without a mark, Franny had nothing. If Elmo and AJ were defrauding someone, then that still didn't explain why Kole met his maker or who perpetrated the crime.

The more I thought of it, the less I believed her. She was all over the place.

"Tell me, Franny. Where were you the night your brother died?"

She swallowed.

"I can't believe you've asked me that. I was in a bar around the corner from here called Flannigan's."

16

FROM THE OUTSIDE, Flannigan's bar appeared much like any other drinking joint I'd ever walked into and its interior didn't disappoint. A long counter and a row of barflies, a clutch of tables, and a pinball machine to attract the younger members of the liquor-consuming fraternity.

The barman wore a shirt and slacks and busied himself shining a glass within an inch of its life. I stood between two men who appeared to have their elbows welded to the bar as they chose not to move one iota as I stepped toward the counter.

"Scotch, please."

The barkeep nodded and poured a shot into a grubby container. The clientele didn't seem to mind they drank from dirty tumblers. They were connoisseurs, after all. I blew a layer of dirt off the top of my drink and took a sip. Watered down, but not so much that you'd notice if you were on your third or fourth. I was stone-cold sober and had consumed my fair share of booze over the years. Fighting in Korea will do that to a man.

I threw some green on the bar and the note was whisked away and replaced with my change. I picked up everything and dropped a healthy tip down so that I could get some attention from the barman. He peered at me and I glanced to my left at a point where the barflies had thinned out. He wandered over to meet me.

"Hey, Mac, I don't suppose you know Franny Kennard."

"Who's asking?"

My badge blinked in the light of day. The guy's eyes widened for a second and I figured he'd mistaken my tin for a detective's shield. I chose not to confuse him with the truth of my profession.

"What does this woman look like?"

I described her hair and mousy disposition.

"I don't recall anyone of that description coming in here."

"Are you sure? She says she's a regular."

He scratched his temple and shook his head. I couldn't decide if he was itchy or had actually attempted to remember his customers.

"Are you on the day shift and someone else works nights? Like Flannigan, maybe?"

Now he clawed at his skull for real. The blankness of his expression told me he had no idea what I was talking about.

"Flannigan? Who's he?"

I blinked.

"The guy the bar is named after."

Pete laughed at me.

"There hasn't been a Flannigan in this joint for twenty years. The old man died before VJ Day."

"And you run it now?"

"Me and the cockroaches."

Despite myself, I glanced down to check for tough-shelled insects.

"Listen, bud, this isn't the place where women come by themselves for a drink. At least, not the sort of woman you've probably been talking to."

"In normal times, she'd most likely be with her brother, Elmo."

His irises expanded a touch. There was recognition in that face.

"I don't know anybody of that moniker. A brother and sister? Nope, we don't have anyone like that round here. How sure are you that you've got the right gin joint?"

It was a fair question, but Franny knew the name of her own bar. She wasn't that much of a flake. What did the barman have to hide?

"Did you say Elmo?"

A rasping voice entered our conversation without an invitation. The barkeep shot a glance at the nearest barfly, six feet away. I took a couple of steps toward him.

"That I did. Do you know him?"

"How well does a fella know any man?"

I sighed. This would not be easy. Talking to drunks never is.

"Well enough to share a drink with him?"

The barfly smiled.

"Share a drink with me, and I'll tell you all I got."

"Now, Hank. Don't go bothering this gentleman with your tall tales."

I looked back at the barman and returned my gaze to Hank.

"I'll buy a glass of whatever he's having."

"Mighty kind, stranger."

"The name's Jake and you're Hank."

The sot attempted to hold out a hand for shaking but realized he would lose his balance if he succeeded. I saved him from the danger of falling off his stool and patted him on the shoulder.

"Pleased to meet you."

"Straight back at ya."

He raised his current beer glass to acknowledge my purchase of his next drink.

"What do you want to know?"

"We were talking about Elmo. You sounded as though you'd met him before. Is that right?"

"I like to speak to folks. That much is true."

"And have you spoken with him or his sister, Franny?"

"I couldn't help but spot your badge earlier. Is there a reward for information that leads to finding these missing people?"

"What makes you believe they've vanished?"

"A flatfoot comes into a bar seeking a man and a woman. Are you telling me that there isn't any financial compensation, Jake?"

"Hank, stop leading the fella astray."

I raised a hand to silence the barman.

"If you tell me something useful to me, then there may be some beer money for you. Depends on how good your tidbits are."

The man pondered for a spell, staring at his drink, head rocking back and forth an inch in each direction. Either he was having a minor stroke or he was deep in thought. Both were possible.

"I reckon I've seen them."

"In here?"

"Yep."

"Hank, have they been in here or not?"

"I think they might have."

"You don't sound very certain."

"Listen, Jake. When you spend your days in this joint, after a while, everyone appears the same, and every day turns into the next. I'm not proud of what I do, but I know who I am."

That last part made little sense to me, but Hank had sat up straight when he said it, so it meant something important to him. And who am I to criticize? I described Franny again in case he hadn't been eavesdropping well enough earlier on.

"I've seen a woman like that in this place."

"Recently?"

"There have been plenty of women in this bar, haven't there, Pete?"

The barman shrugged and resumed cleaning the same glass he had been working on when I arrived in the drinking hole. But he remained within earshot.

"I'm only interested in the woman I've just described to you. Has she been in lately?"

"With a fella?"

"That's right, Hank. With Elmo. On Sunday night."

"I watched them kiss in the booth over there."

His thumb waved in a vague direction toward the back of the bar.

"Kissing? They're brother and sister."

"Oh." Hank lifted the beer to his mouth and finished the glass. Pete removed the receptacle and placed the drink I'd purchased under Hank's nose.

"Sister, you say? Then it can't have been them. It must've been the other two."

I raised my eyes to heaven and on the way down, I caught Pete's expression. He was right. Hank would never make a star witness in a trial, but all I wanted him to do was corroborate Franny's story.

"Apart from the pair kissing, can you recall any other women who were in the bar this weekend?"

"They were cute."

"Who were?"

"The brother and sister."

"What makes you say that?"

"The way they were canoodling in the booth."

I sighed. "You're talking about that other couple again. We're only interested in Franny and Elmo Kennard."

"I'm sure you are."

A short beer was needed. This was going to take longer than I wanted and I needed a little something to keep me from running out of the joint screaming. The drink was delivered by Pete's smirk in less than a minute. I threw a bill onto the counter.

"Ain't you buying me another drink?"

"Hank, you haven't even started the last one I bought you, and I told you I pay for useful information, not the ramblings of a man stuck to a bar counter."

He looked hurt, and I wondered if I should have curtailed my displeasure more. If Pete hadn't been so evasive, I would never have wasted this much energy on this drunk. I tried for what I hoped would be the last time.

"Hank, have you seen a woman in this bar these past few days who matches Franny's description?"

A nod.

"When?"

"Two nights ago. I know it wasn't last night, because that was when Pete told me to leave before he closed up."

"You were getting too boisterous, weren't you, Hank?"

Another nod.

"But the evening before, there was a rare event for Flannigan's Bar."

"How so?"

"Two women in one day? And both pretty? I'd say that was a cause for a celebration."

"You say both appeared at night. Are you certain it wasn't in daylight hours?"

"I can't be certain. I drink too much to be clear about all the details of the world around me, but I sure as hell recollect the two in the booth and the woman on her own."

He described Franny well enough for me to believe she was there.

"And she had no company?"

"Nope, not that I recall, but she kept making calls on the phone."

His thumb made another valiant attempt at indicating a particular direction and failed dismally. Luckily for me, my eyes were working perfectly because there was a phone sitting behind the bar that Pete was now trying to stand in front of.

"Pete, was there a dame in here on Sunday night who asked to make a call?"

"I don't recall."

I stuffed five dollars into Hank's top pocket and tipped my hat. Whatever the reason for the barman being so unhelpful, he sure was succeeding.

17

I DECIDED IT was time to visit South Fifth Plaza again. When I arrived, there was no black sedan in sight, so I parked outside to ensure everyone on the other side of the street could settle in for the show. Then I headed to the entrance to discover whether AJ was receiving visitors.

Within a minute, she had opened the door and her face deflated as soon as she saw me.

"Were you expecting somebody else?"

"Not at all, Mr. Adkins."

"I do wish you'd call me Jake."

"If it will stop you from haranguing me over the matter yet again, then I shall do so in the future."

With that settled, she invited me in and we sat down in the living room.

"I figured you might want an update."

"That I've not been arrested is all I need to know, wouldn't you say?"

"Well, when you put it like that."

"But I do, Mr.… Jake. I paid you an amount of money to achieve a stated goal. I do not care to hear about what you haven't done. All that matters to me is that the outcome happens."

"The DA's head needs turning, and it is going to require a substantive effort."

"I hope this isn't a prelude to a request for further payment. You agreed to a fixed rate for this task and I do not intend to offer you one red cent more."

I fell into silence. This was not how I imagined AJ would respond to my arrival. Most clients find comfort in hearing how I've got on so far. It gives them a sense of progress and hope that I will get the job done.

"The difficulty is that there are conflicting stories about what happened that night and the motivation of certain of the players. I'm hoping you'll share your knowledge of some of these matters."

She fumbled for a smoke and I leaped out of my armchair to light her cigarette. For this effort, I received a half-smile and a thank you.

"How well do you know Elmo Kennard's sister?"

That question was dripping with implications and I was proud of constructing it with little notice. I could be a smart cookie when I put my mind to it.

"Whatever do you mean?"

"Elmo Kennard is in your circle of friends, right?"

She bit her bottom lip and took a long drag on her cigarette.

"I know him. What has he got to do with anything?"

"To be honest, AJ, I was hoping you were going to tell me."

Silence.

"He had nothing to do with my killing Kole."

"Was he with you that evening?"

"What? No. Why would he have been with us on Sunday night?"

"That's what I am trying to figure out. I've spoken with his sister."

I let the statement hang in the air to see how AJ reacted. Ice cool. I made a mental note not to play poker with her if the opportunity ever arose.

"Franny?"

"So you know her."

"Not really. Elmo has mentioned her in passing, but she and I never met."

"Have you corresponded?"

"Now you are toying with me, Jake."

"Oh?"

"I received a strange letter from her last week, but it was the ravings of a disturbed mind and I threw it away. How did you come to know about it?"

"Far be it for me to reveal my professional secrets, but you hired me for a specific outcome and I am doing my best to achieve that goal."

I smiled to myself, but some of my smugness must have oozed out as AJ raised an eyebrow at my words.

"The existence of the letter might give the police second thoughts about your confession. As we both know, Franny threatened Kole's life and a few days later, he was dead."

"You haven't informed them of this development?"

"Keeping the cops in the dark helps me shed light on matters at hand faster than if I run round and blurt out everything I know at the earliest opportunity."

"You mean you tend not to get paid any bonus if your clients see officers of the law tidying up after you?"

"Something like that. Besides, sometimes I can do things the cops can't, or at least they find hard to do without filling out a pile of paperwork."

"Like searching through a woman's trash."

"It was on the sidewalk, which meant it was fair game for anyone walking past."

"But that person was you."

The corner of my mouth curled upwards. She spotted the angles almost before I'd laid out my hand.

"Back to the letter itself. I've met Franny and I agree she does not appear the most stable horse in town. And her alibi is shaky."

"You have been busy, Jake."

"Just doing my job, ma'am. The tricky thing is that I can imagine her doing for Kole, especially as she threatened she would. Franny might have a screw loose, but she had some kind of motive, definitely the means, and not much of an alibi."

AJ dragged on her cigarette.

"And if I'm only half right about her, that makes me want to know why you wish to frame yourself."

She stubbed the butt into her ashtray.

"Jake, you must believe me when I tell you I killed Kole. Elmo was always concerned about Franny's state of mind. He told me on countless occasions, but it doesn't mean she murdered my husband. I did that and you are being paid to prove it so the DA stops thinking it was voluntary manslaughter."

That was a phrase that I had never uttered in front of AJ, but here she was using technical legal jargon. Most civilians can't tell the difference between manslaughter and homicide, let alone slice the former into its constituent pieces.

"Would it not help you if we found sufficient evidence against Franny Kennard?"

"Not at all. I told you I want my day in court and that is with me being the accused. I may be a grieving widow, but I want my confession taken seriously."

A tear fell from her eyes and I moved over to sit next to her on the couch. She seemed so vulnerable at that moment. I pulled out the handkerchief from my jacket and wiped away the salty liquid which had gathered on her cheek.

She took my hand in hers and held it gently for a second before placing it on her lip. I inhaled her perfume and enjoyed the experience. AJ sure was fragrant at that moment. The woman before me leaned in with her mouth only inches away from mine. If I'd stretched my neck a little, we would have been kissing. Perhaps she read my mind.

"There's something I want to show you."

She planted a brief peck on my lips and stood up. I followed her out of the room and up the stairs. As she headed to the second floor, I reminded myself how much I was attracted to her.

⸻ ⸻

IN THE MASTER bedroom, AJ opened up a set of drawers. After a few seconds of rummaging, she gave up the search for the unknown item. She turned to face me and placed a hand on my cheek. I drew her to me and we kissed again.

Only three feet from the bed, I wondered what I was doing and whether I should encourage us to head toward the mattress. Then Veronica's image flashed before my eyes.

She was the woman I was in bed with the night my partner, Ed, got his. It should have been me in that vehicle doing the overnight surveillance job, but I preferred to lie to him and spend the evening under the sheets with his wife, rather than sipping coffee in a car in the middle of a darkened street.

"What's the matter, Jake?"

"Terrible memories of days gone by."

She placed her palms on my cheeks to help me focus on her. Her eyes pierced my soul and her hair smelled exquisite. Then Ed's face popped into my head. I blinked to shake it off, but no good. It was still there.

A bead of sweat appeared on my top lip. AJ looked at me and let go of my cheeks. I tried to smile, but all I could summon was a bizarre grimace. She stepped back, and I strode out of the room and ran down the stairs. Those curves might be in all the right places but I couldn't see my way to do more than look at them from afar without summoning the ghost of Ed Schwartz.

18

I HAD SPENT four long years doing my best to forget my time in Chicago, how Ed died, and his wife who walked out on me soon thereafter. To clear my head, I drove back toward my office and stopped at a diner for a coffee and a piece of cheesecake in Ed's memory.

After I had placed my order, I searched around for a spell and settled into a newspaper I'd found in the adjacent empty booth. With the sports section completed, I was about to tuck into my key lime cake when a woman loomed over me, causing a shadow on the paper. I looked up and my jaw lowered faster than a whore's panties.

"How are you, Jake?"

A blink to make sure I wasn't dreaming.

"I was only thinking about you less than an hour ago."

"Are you going to ask me to sit down?"

"Of course, please do."

I beckoned at the seating, and Veronica Schwartz smiled and sat down opposite me. The waitress hustled over to allow Veronica to order a coffee.

"I'm surprised to find you this far west, Jake. You always told me that Chicago would be your home for life."

"Times change, Veronica."

"Did you leave or were you pushed?"

"It's a complicated story and I won't bore you with it now. How long have you been in LA?"

"Ever since I left the Windy City."

Her eyes gazed into her lap as we both gathered our thoughts around Ed's death. I sighed.

"I knew you headed over to the West Coast, but I had no idea you'd wind up here."

"What's so special about this place?"

"Not the diner. My office is only four blocks away. We've probably passed each other countless times over the years."

"Maybe, Jake. Are you still a private dick?"

"Yes. Different town, same old story."

"Do you have a new partner?"

"Oh no. I've not had one since Ed."

"You're all alone in the city of angels."

"And how about you, Veronica?"

"It took me a while to settle down. In my first year in LA, I moved three or four times. But now I'm happy where I am in Pasadena."

"So this isn't your neighborhood?"

"Not at all. I've visited a friend and figured I'd pop into this place for a drink before I headed back home."

"What are the chances, eh?"

"I know. It is a small world, Jake Adkins."

She grinned at me and I was pleased we had both picked this joint of all the others in the area.

"It's good to see you again. I'd forgotten how much your smile can lift my heart."

"You always knew how to say all the right things, Jake."

"And I meant them too."

"In the moment, for sure, but those were different times. We were younger back in the day."

"You haven't aged a day, Veronica."

I extracted another smile from her.

"It's kind of you to mention, but we both know that isn't true."

I shook my head to disagree but didn't press the point, because she was right. She had added a few pounds, and I noticed a wrinkle above her nose that had not been there when we were last in the same room together. But that did not matter to me. I glanced at her wedding finger and noted there was no ring.

That surprised me because I remembered Veronica as the sort of woman who always wanted a man around. For the companionship. I had imagined her hightailing it to be as far away from me and Ed's death as she could, and marrying the first eligible bachelor she bumped into. It shows what a terrible judge of her character I had been.

"Are you working on a case at the minute, or are you between jobs?"

"I'm eating this cheesecake on a client's dime."

We laughed.

"I bet it tastes good."

"Sure does. Want to try?"

I offered a small forkful and Veronica leaned in to scoop up the mouthful with her tongue. I had forgotten how much she stirred me and then it all came flooding back. The nights while Ed was out working. The stolen afternoons when I was supposed to be wading through paperwork. Motel rooms...

"What are you thinking?"

"I'm remembering the afternoons and evenings we spent together."

Her cheeks reddened.

"They were the best of times and the worst of times."

"Thanks."

"I was referring to Ed's murder."

"Yes, of course. Sorry."

"It's not all about you, Jake."

"I know."

On this occasion, it was my cheeks that heated up, but Veronica's smile extinguished my embarrassment. She could still calm my beating heart. I polished off the remains of the cheesecake and the waitress came over to clear the crockery.

"Do you want anything else?"

I glanced at Veronica, hoping she'd order another drink.

"Would you like something, Veronica?"

"No, I'm good, thanks."

I tried to hide my disappointment. Even though we were still sitting at the table, I was missing her already.

"My apartment is nearby. Do you fancy a coffee or something a bit stronger?"

She glanced at her watch as if she had a train to catch.

"Yes, that would be nice. But I can only stay a short while. I've got a thing to go to at five."

As far as I was concerned, that gave us several hours.

***

I PROVIDED VERONICA with the address, but she followed me in her car anyway. As we waited at the elevator, I thought how her skirt suit was quite formal for a visit to a friend. In the apartment, we wandered into the living room and she sat on my couch.

"Coffee?"

"You mentioned liquor."

I opened the drinks cabinet and stated the options available.

"A sherry would be pleasant."

I poured a sensible measure for Veronica and a shot of Scotch for myself. We clinked our glasses, and both took a sip. Sitting next to the woman, I eyed her from the tip of her toes in her dainty blue shoes up to the top of her head. Whatever it was, she still had it.

"Do you work or has the life insurance been keeping you afloat?"

"I get by, Jake."

"Pleased to hear it, although, by the look of you, you're doing more than merely scraping along."

Another smile and Veronica took a second sip of the sherry.

"A girl does what she must to survive in this world."

"If you don't mind me asking, are you going steady with anyone?"

She laughed.

"Since when has something like that mattered to you?"

"Good point. My track record hasn't been great in that regard, I suppose."

"Not at all, Jake."

"Although to be fair to myself, I saw no one else when we were seeing each other."

"I'd have known if you did. If you weren't with me, you were with Ed. You had no spare time to spend with anybody else."

"You got me there, Veronica."

I placed my palm on her knee for a second. We both stared at what I had done and I removed it almost as soon as I had touched the material of her skirt. She patted my hand and gave it a squeeze.

"Are you going to show me the whole of your mansion?"

"Where are my manners?"

I pointed out the kitchenette and the bathroom. Then the only other room, off the hallway, was the bedroom. I hesitated for a second and then led her in.

"If I had known I was having visitors, I'd have tidied the place up."

I grabbed some clothes from the floor and stuffed them into the wardrobe while Veronica laughed at me.

"It's a bachelor's life for you. If this is how you leave your home, I can tell that you're not seeing anyone at the moment."

My cheeks heated up and my tongue squirmed around my mouth, unable to help me form a syllable, let alone reply.

"That's all right, Jake. I'm only teasing you."

She stepped toward me and I stroked her cheek with the back of my palm. She raised her hand and rested it on my upper arm, smiling. I leaned in to kiss her and she licked her lips.

Then the most extraordinary thing in the world happened. The image of Ed's bullet-addled body flashed through my mind, and I paused. The blood drained from Veronica's cheek as I touched it. It went cold under my fingers and I realized she'd experienced the same horrendous flashback too.

We stepped back from each other and I pretended to tidy up the items left sprawling on the dressing table. She pivoted on a pin and strode out of the room, fussing with her hair and muttering something about the time.

"I'd better be going."

"Yes, I understand."

Another one of those melting smiles. She pecked me on the cheek and headed for the door. By the time I had tried to catch up, she had reached the top of the stairwell; she didn't wait for the elevator and give me a chance to speak to her or anything else.

For two weeks, I made that diner my go-to place, but I never saw Veronica Schwartz again.

19

I TOOK A cold shower to clear my head and as I pushed my arm through my shirt sleeve, I realized I was looking for answers in the wrong place. In Los Angeles, whenever there's a fraud, it involves either land or water. The people who have made it to the other side of the country don't fall for non-existent bridges or the promise of a big win on the horses.

And where there's a scam involving land or water, then there are legal-looking documents to accompany the play. These pieces of paper tend not to collect dust lying in someone's house or apartment. They are lodged at the County Clerk's office in Norwalk and that was where I was headed.

The facade was that of every other gray municipal building you have ever checked out and ignored. But to me, there was a treasure trove inside. I skipped to the reception table and explained my visit to the young lady, who directed me to the second floor.

If the entranceway was drab, then the Land Records department had all the remaining color sucked out of it. A monochrome man with wiry glasses perched on the end of his nose sat at the main desk and ignored me. I tried a polite cough, but this did nothing. After a further excruciating half-minute, he pointed at a bell ten inches from where he was reading and then retracted his finger.

I dinged the instrument and still, he continued to read. Five long seconds later, he looked up.

"Yes?"

"I'm hoping you can help me."

"I'm sure you are."

Was he being willful with me in particular, or did he behave this way to everyone he met? If it was the latter, then it would explain why he was working in the black-and-white Records Department. A small piece of me died inside. I glanced around his desk and noticed his brass nameplate on a wooden triangular prism in front of him. Andrew Bechingham.

"Andrew. Andy. I'm seeking recent records about land or water transactions."

He tapped his name sign.

"Mr. Bechingham, if you don't mind."

"My apologies. Would you be able to provide me with access to those documents, please?"

He sighed and pulled out a notepad from the top drawer of his desk.

"How far back do you wish to go?"

"Twelve months should be fine, thank you."

"Across the entire county, or can you narrow matters down?"

"Cast the net as wide as possible."

"We are on a fishing expedition, I see."

Andy wasn't wrong, but Franny had been so sure that AJ and Elmo were involved in a scam and the sister had a far from secure alibi. Something was up and I wanted to get to the bottom of it.

"How long do you believe it will take you to find all the paperwork?"

He glanced at his watch again. Was he bored with the conversation or was he about to go on a break?

"Give me thirty minutes. You can wait over there."

His pointing finger indicated a wooden bench with little cushioning that I could see from this distance.

"I'll grab a drink and be back in a while."

"Ahem."

Bechingham tapped another sign on his desk using the end of his pen. I needed to pay the access fee before the pinhead did anything.

Ten dollars later, I had the receipt in my pocket and I stood on the street with a coffee in my hand.

By this point in my life, my blood must have been pure caffeine, because I was never more than five minutes away from my next cup. I leaned against a low wall around the corner from the County Clerk's office and watched the world go by. I was surprised the pretzel concession where I'd bought my coffee hadn't gone bust years ago; there were so few people on the sidewalk.

"How's business?"

"Never been better."

"That I can see."

"It's the wrong time of day, Mac. You should see this place when the worker bees come to the hive in the morning and leave in the evening. That's when I make my money."

"Pleased to hear it. Mighty fine cup of java."

A while later, I glanced at my watch and threw the remnants of my drink into the trash.

Back to Bechingham's floor and the mono-man was at his desk, reading. I knew better than to cough in his presence, and I pinged the bell. He glanced up in an instant and almost smiled at me, but it came out more as a sneer. Of course, that could have been the expression he was aiming for.

Andrew stood up and led me to a room off the main corridor. As he opened the door, there were more Manila folders visible than I had ever witnessed before in my life.

"There you go. Don't take any of the paperwork out of here. We shut at five.

———

SOMEWHERE BENEATH THE sea of papers was a desk, and I sat down. Where to begin? From the right and over to the left. The search for any document with the Langchamp or Kennard name upon it. That was all I needed, so the good news was that I didn't need to spend much time on any individual piece of paper.

A glance at the bottom of each of the final pages showed me who had signed each document and, time after time, that was enough for it to be added to the reject pile.

After a couple of hours, I had nothing to show for my effort other than an enormous mound of folders that I had opened and found wanting. There were only about another ten inches of files to wade through before my task was complete and showed to be futile.

Three-quarters of the way through the rest I reached the moment when I wondered if there weren't better ways for me to spend my afternoon. Two documents later and I discovered the warm glow that you only get when you've been proved right against the odds.

The door remained shut, but I stared at it for a second anyway. I pulled out the two pages from their Manila folder, bent them in half, and stuffed them inside my jacket. If there were other secrets to be discovered, I had enough on my person to suit my purposes and I'd no desire to remain in that musty cell any longer than I had to.

Out the door, I glanced over toward Bechingham, who was still reading at his desk. I considered telling him I was off, but then I figured he'd count every sheet that was in the folders to ensure I hadn't taken any. The man had a terrifying eye for detail.

20

I SHOVED MY hands in my pants pockets and padded along the sidewalk. Just before I put my hand on the handle of my car, I realized I hadn't had a sniff of a coffee since before my stint in the reading room.

A quick one-eighty and I headed over to the same concession I'd been to before. A good drink and the guy had been pleasant. As I walked over, I thought to myself that the morning and evening commuter crowd must be quite something to see, as there was still nobody on the streets.

"I'm back again."

"Java?"

"You bet, Mac."

"Call me Jake. All my friends do."

"I'm Bert."

The guy poured my coffee, and we chatted some more about nothing in particular. Then I bade him farewell and aimed for my vehicle. Although it should have been no surprise by now, the sidewalk remained devoid of people and I sauntered toward my car, only half a block away. I took a sip from my drink and a pink sports car flew past. Cute shape, terrible color. The guy'd better watch out or a cop will pull him over for poor taste and high speed. There was no way he was traveling under the limit.

Four hundred feet to go. I peered into my coffee and found there was half a cup remaining. Another swig polished off most of the remains. My jalopy stood on its own by the curb, as though all the other vehicles that had been near it when I parked had had a falling out and left the vicinity.

Two hundred feet. I caught an engine sound from behind. I glanced back hoping it was another chichi vehicle, but it was a boring black number. Never mind. Another sip and the vehicle got louder and a thump sounded as a tire mounted the sidewalk. I glanced behind, and the sedan headed straight at me, a handful of feet from my heels.

I hit the dirt and rolled away from the road so that my body was wedged by the building. The car sped past and returned to its lane. My coffee cup remained in my hand, but its contents splatted on the paving slabs. That could have been my brain.

Letting go of the receptacle, I scrambled to get to my jalopy, fumbling for the keys, and then I gunned the engine to catch up with whoever it was had decided I must die.

* * *

THE SALOON REVVED at least three blocks ahead of me and hadn't slowed down since its failed attempt at sending me to my maker. I pressed my foot to the floor as I tried to reduce the gap between us.

It slowed down to swing right, and I maintained my speed until the last second. The difference between me and the other driver was that I'd been in this kind of situation before and the other guy operated at an amateur level.

At that moment, I realized I didn't know whether a man or a woman sat at the wheel. Everything had happened so fast, but there had been a reflection on the front windscreen, so I hadn't had a good look at the driver when I glanced back.

Two blocks behind and the sedan swerved around the upcoming cars, each screech reassuring me they were not in full control of their vehicle. I flitted in and out of the traffic and gained another half-block. They were too far away for me to even see the driver's head, let alone identify my would-be assailant.

A truck pulled into my lane without warning and I slammed on my brakes and veered out of the way. The sedan remained visible ahead, but that maneuver had cost me vital seconds.

I blinked, and the sedan was gone. My fist slammed the steering wheel in frustration. Then I blinked again and there it was, still three blocks ahead. I sighed and pumped the gas pedal to squeeze as much as I could out of my old jalopy. Luck was on my side because my lane became eerily empty, whereas the car in front was zigzagging its way around the traffic.

Within a few seconds, I had made yardage and was only two blocks away. Still too far to do much good, but it was an improvement. And the longer I maintained the pressure, the harder for the amateur to keep focus. The years of experience as a private eye were paying off now.

Another right by the car up ahead and a smoother turn by me, and there was only a block between us. So far, the lights had been green all the way, but then the situation changed when a red appeared. The driver ahead hit the brake on instinct and that helped me catch up half a block because I was not constrained by anything.

They must have seen me in their rear-view mirror because the sedan lurched forward as they touched the gas again and, with nobody to get in the way, they floored it and zoomed through the lights. As I arrived at the same junction, everything went green and I shot through, weaving between the once-stationary vehicles.

I was close enough to see the back of the driver's head, but not so near that I could identify any of their features. No hair length or color. Nothing that would help me find out who it was that wanted me dead.

The road ahead was clear and, for the first time since I gave chase, the sedan took a left and I followed. This street was narrower, with only one lane each way, and the traffic got heavier. Poor decision, my friend.

I gained fifty feet by reading the movement of the cars better than the other driver, who was still swerving left and right to make any yardage. The trick is to lean back in your seat, arms straight but relaxed, and spot the space that will open up when the vehicles in front continue to move at their current speed. It's like playing pool on a table that is constantly tilting in different directions.

A smile formed on my face as I knew the longer we remained on this street, the easier it would be for me to get to them. Three hundred feet. Then, to my dismay, they turned right just before the lights changed. I sped through the red and hounded the sedan again. It took another right half a block along and we zoomed through an alleyway behind the office buildings.

With inches to spare on either side, the car in front slowed down a touch, but I knew that when you were driving straight ahead, it didn't matter what you were motoring past. I maintained my pace and found myself only two hundred feet behind.

Out of the alleyway and we both lucked out, as there was nothing to interrupt our high-speed journey as we shot out onto the main drag. My assailant had gained confidence since our last trip along a four-lane highway and speeded up a notch, gliding past cars. I kept my eyes focused hard on its shiny rear bumper and did everything I could to decrease the distance between us. One hundred feet.

This was the point when I eyed up what was happening either side of the vehicle ahead. Thoughts of how to take it off the road flickered through my concentration, and that was my downfall.

The approaching lights displayed green and had been for some time, which meant only one thing was inevitable. The sedan zoomed through as the colors changed before me and I was so fixated on following them I failed to notice a lorry coming in from the right.

I stamped on the brake and he did too as our vehicles inched nearer and nearer. The one thing that flashed through my mind was how big the explosion would be if I hit the oncoming gas truck.

This was the motivation I needed to hard-lock the steering wheel so that I careered past the truck's front bumper, missing the potential ball of flames by two inches. The sedan sped away, and I halted, knowing that this escapade had stolen any opportunity I might have had to catch up with whoever was sitting behind the wheel.

As I listened to the angry tirade of the truck driver, I wondered who wanted to mow me down. It could have been an ex-girlfriend or one of their husbands. I have never been too particular about the marital status of the women I've slept with.

21

AFTER I EXTRICATED myself from the argument with the truck driver, I couldn't decide if I needed a coffee or hard liquor. I split the difference back in the office by brewing up a pot of my favorite brown liquid and adding a healthy dash of Scotch to the mug.

Sylvia popped her head around the door once she sensed I had settled into my chair.

"How are things going with Mrs. Langchamp?"

"Now that is an excellent question, my dear."

She smiled in response. I reminded myself to praise her more often. My habit is to always pick on people's faults and not acknowledge when they've done something right or well. That is one reason I've gone through so many secretaries over the years. Sylvia hovered by the door.

"Sit down, why don't you? I'd be interested in your take on the situation."

The first thing I did was to describe my near-death experience behind the wheel. She gasped when she heard how close I had been to smashing into the gas truck.

"You're fortunate to be alive, Jake."

"I'm never sure about that, but it was a lucky escape."

"And you say you didn't get a good look at who tried to run you over?"

"Not at all. In all the excitement, I had no time to read the license plate."

"Shame."

She slumped back in her chair. This gal cared.

"What did you find out in the Clerk's office?"

"That I can answer. There were two deeds issued in the last month. Both had Kole and A.J. Langchamp's signatures."

"How does that prove they were caught up in any fraud?"

"The addresses are places owned by Jack Dragna and there is no way anyone in this case is involved with that man."

Sylvia blinked at me and attempted to switch on a knowing smile but failed.

"For your information, Dragna runs Los Angeles for the mob. The deeds relate to venues of a salacious reputation that underpin his gaming and prostitution empire."

"And those are subjects about which you possess a vast knowledge, Jake."

"No need to get smart, Sylvia. Let's just say that in my line of work, you meet all sorts along the way. Including the likes of Dragna."

I had only met him once, and that was enough for a lifetime. The fella oozed power out of every pore and had a presence that meant everyone felt uncomfortable being in the same room. Nobody messed with Jack Dragna. If he knew AJ and Kole were pretending to sell off his real estate, then they'd be buried in the desert by now, or languishing in the foundations of a new building.

"But, Jake, if the two were scamming someone, why would AJ kill her accomplice?"

"That piece I haven't fathomed yet, but the key lies with Franny, who had figured out there was a fraud going on, but thought it involved her brother, Elmo. I only encountered the guy one time, but he didn't give me the impression of being a criminal mastermind."

"He might be a talented actor."

"Elmo seemed too eager to please. If it wasn't me, then it was his neighbor. And Franny thinks the world of him. Her letter to AJ was confused but she recognized Kole was a threat to Elmo's happiness with AJ."

"You reckon deep down, she knew that Kole and AJ were involved in the fraud?"

"Franny does an excellent job of making everybody believe she is so ditzy, but I don't buy the act. Her home was untidy but clean. Nothing seemed to occupy a place of its own, but there was no dust on any of the ornaments, no splashes left to dry on the floor. She is far more together than she lets people believe."

"With all this going on, Jake, why did AJ confess to the murder? Wouldn't she have been better off running away or pinning the blame on Franny Kennard?"

"If I had the answer to that question, then this would all be sewn up, and I'd have earned my fee."

Sylvia smiled and poured herself a coffee. I noticed her glance at my liquor bottle, but she chose not to add any to her mug. She strolled back to her seat and I reminded myself how easy she was on the eye.

When she sat down, Sylvia crossed her legs and I felt a warmth in the pit of my stomach. That feeling was usually reserved for a good hunch on the winner of a horse race or the sight of an attractive woman.

"How are you finding life not being in a couple?"

Her expression showed she couldn't figure out how I knew, and then she remembered our chat the other night.

"He'll be fine once he gets used to the idea."

"I was thinking about you, silly."

Sylvia's cheeks heated up.

"Oh, I was the one who split us up, so I'd already had time to get accustomed to the whole notion before it ended."

"What happened?"

"It's my own fault, really, Jake. I have this habit of dating guys who look great, but don't have too much going on upstairs."

She sighed.

"You deserve a more cerebral man."

"Do you have anybody in mind?"

I smiled and sipped my drink before responding. As I parted my lips to speak, Sylvia interrupted me before I began.

"Jake, I'd like a thinker next, but he mustn't be buried in his books. Someone with a better balance. Every time I date a hunk, the first few weeks are fun, but we don't have a thing to talk about after the initial…"

"Passion?"

"Uh-huh. Once the passion subsides, you know?"

"I can imagine that, for sure."

I may not know much about anything, but I've learned over the years that the best way to a woman's heart is through your ears. Listen to her and she'll be a stayer, but the minute your mind wanders, then you should bet your last dime that you'll split up within a week.

A gulp and I took a chance to ask the most important question of the night.

"Sylvia, would you be free some time for us to share a drink under more social circumstances?"

I waved my hand at the contents of the office to imply that we could carry on here or go somewhere more like a bar. I did my best to feign not caring about the outcome of my inquiry. Sylvia bit her lower lip and I prepared for disappointment.

"Jake, I don't mind if I do."

She puffed out her chest under her suit jacket and I punched the air, but only in my head. There is nothing lovelier than dating the woman you work with. You leave at the same time and you do not waste energy talking about what happened in the office that day.

"Later this week, perhaps?"

She raised her eyes to concentrate on her imaginary diary.

"That sounds like a fabulous idea, Jake."

"Tomorrow?"

"That's a plan."

We both smiled and sipped at our drinks. After the encounters I'd had the previous couple of days, it would be good to be near a woman and not suffer images of Ed Schwartz spinning around my brain. This would be a guilt-free date.

"There's one thing I haven't mentioned, Sylvia."

"Oh?" The suspicion in her voice was palpable.

"About the case."

"I see." Her shoulders relaxed.

"There was an address on a torn scrap of paper I found in AJ's that didn't chime."

"How so?"

"It was in Malibu and that is not where the Langchamps or the Kennards live. I think it means something, but I have no idea what that might be."

"A new clue. How exciting."

"A forgotten lead, until now, at any rate."

My emphasis was aimed as a jibe at me, but Sylvia seemed deflated.

"I should have thought about it earlier."

"But you were knee-deep in trash. Don't be so hard on yourself."

"That's why I like you around, Sylvia. You always have something good to say about me."

"You're one smart cookie, Jake Adkins."

"In that case, would you do me a favor?"

She thrust her shoulders back as though she were taking orders in the army.

"Whatever you want."

I shoved a hand in my pants pocket and pulled out my roll, passing a bunch of notes over to my secretary.

"First thing in the morning, would you hop over to a clothing store and buy me a pair of casual slacks and a shirt or two?"

"Shopping?"

"It's time I paid a visit to Malibu."

WEDNESDAY

22

SYLVIA DELIVERED MY new clothes to my apartment, but I didn't invite her in as I wanted to get going. Besides, when I asked her out for a drink, she wouldn't have had in mind a cup of home-brewed java.

Malibu was less than an hour away, but it seemed like a thousand miles. As soon as you leave the city, the greenery engulfs you and it's easy to forget there's more to California than the little town of Los Angeles. When I arrived, I popped into a diner to grab a mug of coffee and also to ask for help. I had an address, but no idea where the place was. Betsy offered some useful advice.

"It's not that far from here. Are you sure you don't want a slice of something sweet?"

I got free directions, so I owed the waitress and ordered a piece of walnut cake.

"We've got a map of the area somewhere. I'll see if I can dig it up."

I waited for Betsy to deliver my drink and a slab of cake. It was big enough for a family of four, but I figured she thought she was being generous. Then she scurried off, and I noticed her shapely ankles and calves. A minute later, she returned with a folded mass of paper.

"Here we are."

She had unfurled the map onto the table, being careful not to knock over my food and drink. A stab at an intersection with her fingertip showed the location of the diner.

"And you want… here."

A finger on her other hand pointed to a place three inches away. Betsy was right; it wasn't that far away. I drank my coffee and left most of the cake, but handed over a large tip.

"Something wrong with the food?"

"Not at all, but it's too early in the morning for me."

She smiled and her eyes widened when she caught sight of the gratuity. I walked from the building free of guilt.

A FEW MINUTES later and I wondered why Betsy hadn't mentioned quite what place she had sent me to. I stopped near the entrance of a trailer park and tried to figure out where I'd find my quarry in the morass of portable homes.

I idled the car along what felt like the main street and got my bearings. Then I parked and walked down one artery until I arrived at the number on the scrap of paper, which was in my pants pocket. I regretted not bringing a jacket; there were so many places I could shove stuff.

When I reached 259, there was no sign of life. I circled the trailer, but no lights were on and nobody stirred. This was the other reason for wishing to wear my jacket; the garment was an easy way to hide my piece and now I felt naked without it.

A knock on the door yielded no result, so I tried the handle. Nada. I peeked into the nearest window and gawped at an empty trailer. Another trip around the place and this time I looked into every window hoping to spot an occupant, but there was nobody to be seen.

I might not have been wearing my jacket, but I still had a small metal file in my wallet and I used that to jimmy open the door. These trailers weren't built with security in mind and with less than ten seconds of effort, I was inside.

The interior comprised a kitchen area which ended in a living space. Next to the sink stood a door that I imagined led to a shower and beyond that was a curtain. I poked my nose through and found the sleeping quarters. You had everything here that you might need to lead a normal life, provided you didn't stretch both your arms out at the same time.

I checked inside a cupboard, discreetly fashioned out of a fake wall, and discovered a man's entire wardrobe. Only no man. Who lived here?

I popped my head out of the door and examined the mailbox. There were three or four letters, which implied the occupant hadn't been round these parts for at least a day or two.

Back inside, I sat down to gather my thoughts. There was a loaf of bread and some jelly in a food cupboard, but the refrigerator was empty, apart from some milk, which would soon transform into a science experiment. Whoever lived here was not a man who ate in this place on a regular basis. Maybe Betsy had served him his meals on his way to and from the trailer park.

Something was wrong in the state of California. This place contained the guy's things, but nothing personal. None of the items that you'd associate with a normal living soul were inside.

I glanced around, my eyes flitting from the kitchen sink to the clothes cupboard, to the bathroom door, and back to the cupboard. I'd almost missed it and only just noticed the wall had a straight line running from top to bottom. That was a hidden door. Perhaps other hidey-holes were waiting to be unearthed.

First thing, I tapped every surface I could find and hoped that I'd hear the hollow thud of a concealed space, but nothing. I returned to the bench seat in the living end of the trailer, a hand resting on a cushion. I squeezed it and thought I felt something hard.

A search in the kitchen drawer revealed a knife and I sliced the cushion open to see what was contained within. Bits of stuffing. This was getting me nowhere. I ran into the bedroom and took the knife to the mattress just in case, but all I saw before me was shredded material and not much else.

With nothing left worth slashing, I replaced the blade in the drawer and sat down facing the clothes cupboard. A light bulb appeared above my head and I flattened my palms against every wall in the place. If there was another hidden space, then I would find it.

Fifteen minutes later, I stood in the middle of the trailer with nothing to show for my efforts other than a pair of dirty palms. This joint had never been cleaned. I checked the faucet and found the water supply was connected, so I washed my hands.

Then I looked around to find somewhere to dry them. I could find no towel, so I tried the little door under the sink. There was a pile of handcloths, neatly folded. I grabbed one, dried up, and replaced it from where it came.

There had to be something in this place that was important to AJ and I didn't want to leave here empty-handed. I pulled open the kitchen drawer again, but there was only a small selection of silverware and a couple of sharp knives.

I turned round and opened the clothes cupboard for the umpteenth time. Shirts, pants, and two jackets. No underwear. A scowl at the situation and I peered down below for the first time. There was another drawer just above the floor. I kneeled and pulled at its handle, but the thing was stuck.

A yank and the left side edged forward a quarter of an inch. A pull on the right-hand side and it too moved the same amount. I walked the drawer out of its hole, a bit from one side, a smidge of movement from the other, until it popped out and landed with a thump on the floor. Shorts and socks.

I sighed. That hadn't been worth the effort. Indeed, if I had been living the trailer life, then I wouldn't have put up with that every day I got dressed. I picked up the wooden container and let the underwear fall out. An envelope had been taped to the underside. Pay dirt.

The tape peeled away with little effort on my part, as though this was not the first time it had been taken off the bottom of the drawer. The yellow envelope was unsealed, and I emptied its contents onto the table by the bench.

Papers. I sifted through them, careful to keep everything in the same order. There were receipts and invoices dating back to the ark, and a savings account book for Julius Warner. I flipped to the last page with writing on it. The balance stood at ten thousand dollars. Mr. Warner was a man of means who lived in a crummy neighborhood.

To the rear of the pile were the deeds to the trailer with Warner as the sole owner, and a marriage certificate. Julius's wife had a maiden name, which is not that uncommon, but what was rarer was that the name was Avril Langchamp.

23

THE BANK OF Malibu was not hard for me to locate. I stopped at Betsy's diner and used its phone directory to get the location and then I stayed for a java, but no cake this time.

"Did you find the place?"

Betsy was there with the coffeepot before I had a chance to sit down. She remembered my tip from earlier on.

"Yes, thanks. Now I'm off to the center of town."

"You lead a busy life."

"It comes in waves. Some weeks there's nothing to do and other times, like this week, it's full to the brim."

She smiled and poured my java, but I was itching to be on my way.

"I've changed my mind. Can I have that to go, please?"

Her shoulders sagged as she imagined her gratuity evaporating before her eyes, but I left her a dollar to show there were no hard feelings.

***

THE PLACE LOOKED like every other financial institution I'd been in. Imposing stonework on the outside and a large quantity of walnut veneer slapped around the interior. It also had the inevitable marble floor, which is there to remind investors where their money is going. You never bump into a disheveled banker.

In front of me were four tellers, each with their own line. I figured I'd choose the second shortest because the one that seems the fastest rarely proves that way. In less than ten minutes, I stood before a middle-aged woman with horn-rimmed glasses.

"How can I help you today, sir?"

"I am the executor of a will of a customer of yours and I would like to meet the manager to finalize the deceased's estate."

"Do you have an appointment?"

"I'm afraid not, but this meeting need only take a couple of minutes. I wouldn't want to waste the manager's time."

"Wait here and I'll find out for you."

I leaned against the counter. In my dealings with people over the years, I've found that cashiers value hierarchy, because they know they are at the bottom of the heap. So, I tend to reinforce the idea that bank managers are gods and we are mere mortals. To me, everyone's the same. We walk, we talk, we love and we go to the bathroom, although not all of us at the same time.

After a minute's absence, I sensed dagger eyes from those in the line behind me, but it wasn't my fault the teller had left her station. I turned around and smiled at the assortment of people with financial transactions to perform. Nobody appeared to appreciate my acknowledgment of their plight. A lifetime later, the cashier came back.

"Mr. Potter is busy at the moment, but he has a free slot in an hour."

I booked the appointment and left in search of a coffee.

I CHOSE THE steak and fries from a nearby restaurant. It had been a long morning, and I had no idea when I might eat in the evening. There was no point in being out of sorts when Sylvia and I caught up for that drink later.

The food was average, and the meal helped me pass the wait well enough. It was better than being stuck in a diner, eating more coffee and cake. I made a mental note to find other ways to spend time while I waited for the world to catch up with me.

My watch said I was due to return to the bank, so I finished my drink and sauntered back. Now, I didn't wait in line and strode over to a different desk where a man sat, monitoring the room. He had some paperwork in front of him but hadn't touched it from the second I arrived in the joint.

"I'm here to see Mr. Potter. The name's Adkins."

"Take a seat, Mr. Adkins. I'll let him know you are here."

The pace in the bank was still glacial, and the glorified receptionist moved toward a door marked for staff only at such a snail's pace, I thought he might be having a seizure. But no, he just wasn't in a hurry. By the time the guy came back, I had grown a beard.

"Mr. Potter will be with you in a minute."

This was bank code for twenty minutes I discovered more than a quarter of an hour later. The important thing was that after an agonizing wait, I stood in front of Mr. Reginald Potter. His leather armchair was huge, or he was a tiny man. When he got up to shake my hand, I found out that the chair was a normal size.

"My colleague tells me that one of our customers has joined the choir invisible."

I cleared the back of my throat.

"Yes, Julius Warner held his funds in this bank and I am hoping to resolve some matters before we finalize the documentation on his estate."

Potter nodded, and I imagined his little legs dangling from his swivel chair, not quite reaching the floor.

"Do you have his account details, by any chance? It will speed up things at this end."

I proffered the savings book to the high priest of high finance. He thanked me and pressed a button on his squawk box.

"Yes, Mr. Potter?"

"Please, can you provide me with a current statement for Mr. Julius Warner?"

He read out the account number and the disembodied voice promised to get on it right away. I rued the fact that I hadn't brought a book along with me, because they had carried everything else out slower than a centipede can take off his shoes.

While we waited, Reginald attempted to keep me busy through small talk, but he was not playing to his strengths, and I saw no reason to help him out.

"Have you traveled far?"

"From LA."

"And did you know Mr. Warner well?"

"Not at all. You?"

"I'm sorry to say that we never had an opportunity to meet."

"Shame."

I maintained that annoying level of noncommunication going until a young woman knocked and entered the room several minutes later. She passed a sheet of paper over to Potter, who thanked her and perused the missive. While he did that, I enjoyed the view as the secretary left the office.

Meanwhile, Potter held the bank book in one hand and the piece of paper in the other. His eyes darted from one to the next and back again.

"Is there something wrong, Mr. Potter?"

"Not exactly."

He was playing conversational hardball with me now.

"What do you mean?"

"The account details in the bank book are correct. Mr. Warner was indeed a customer, and he held a significant sum with us. Ten thousand dollars, to be precise. So you can include the account within his estate. I will write a letter to that effect for your record."

"That's mighty helpful of you, thanks."

"But there is a small discrepancy on the balance."

"Oh."

"Mr. Potter, what is the nature of the discrepancy?"

He wasn't giving anything away, and I wanted to return to LA some time that day.

"The balance in the book doesn't match the amount in our records."

"Has interest accrued?"

"Nothing like that, Mr. Adkins."

"Then...?"

He stared back at the book and paper but failed to add to his earlier statements. This man would never buckle under a police interrogation. If he wasn't so upright, I'd have advised him to rob a bank.

"Please give us a few minutes, Mr. Adkins, so that we can be sure of the facts."

"Mind if I smoke?"

"Not at all."

He pointed to an ashtray on his table that had two butts languishing in it. I offered him one of mine, but he declined. Instead, he closed a folder on his desk and walked out. Whatever he had to say, wasn't to be conveyed via a squawk box or be heard by me.

I finished my cigarette and lit another. Boredom can be an evil foe. Potter arrived in the room before I had put the second one out. He sat down, clutching a file containing at least ten pieces of paper.

"This is the situation, Mr. Adkins. The balance at the minute is at zero."

"Nothing in the account at all?"

"Not at present. You were correct a minute ago. Interest has accumulated and is due to be added in sixteen days."

"But where has all the money gone?"

"That is not a question I can answer with any ease. A sum was debited on Monday."

"How much for?"

"The entire balance."

Reginald peered at me over the papers he held in his hands. Only a banker would call ten thousand bucks a minor item. Ten large out of the door of the Bank of Malibu without even a flicker of an eyelid. You have to admire people in the bank business.

"Do you have a record of who withdrew the money?"

"Yes, we do."

I waited, but Potter had answered my question and felt no reason to elaborate on any details.

"Who was it?"

"His wife."

24

I CHANGED OUT of my Malibu outfit and returned to a suit, tie, and fedora. Then a short hop to my office, where Sylvia was busy typing something important and fielding calls. To amuse myself, I pretended the phone rang off the hook with interesting potential clients and not bailiffs baying at my heels.

As I'd told Betsy, the private eye business goes in waves. This week was a good one, but I knew there were no bookings after the weekend.

"Any calls this morning?"

"No, Jake. I'm afraid not."

She smiled up at me and I returned the favor. Sylvia had a cute nose.

I stumbled into my inner sanctum and flung myself into my chair. It swung round, and I perched my feet on the radiator and looked out at the City of Angels. If you ignored the traffic and the pollution, it was a beautiful town. I was glad I'd put Chicago behind me.

Sylvia knocked on my door and brought me crashing out of my reverie.

"I'm making a pot. Fancy a brew?"

"That'd be nice. Thank you."

She swanned over to the coffeepot and busied herself until the glug-splutter of the machine doing its work erupted into the room.

Once it fell into silence, she poured two mugs and passed one to me. To the other, she added a level spoonful of sugar.

"I shouldn't, because I'm watching my weight."

"You have no worries on that score, Sylvia. There's nothing wrong with a bit of sweet in your life."

I raised a palm and indicated she was welcome to sit down. With her hands on either side of her mug, that was what she did, crossing her legs as she landed. The client seat was never as comfortable as mine and Sylvia knew this.

"Did you find out anything interesting on your trip to Malibu?

⸺ ⸺

A BROAD GRIN spread across my face and I leaned back in my chair, arms splayed over both armrests.

"I know who killed Kole Langchamp."

"You do? Who?"

"Franny Kennard."

"Weren't we trying to frame our own client and not find some other fall guy?"

"Or gal."

"Are you serious?"

"I sure am."

"How?"

"One of AJ's neighbors saw her on the night of the murder at the Langchamp house. She had threatened Kole's life the week before in a letter to AJ."

"How reliable is the neighbor?"

"I'll admit Gladys Blake's testimony is shaky at best, but taken in the round, I reckon I've closed the case."

"Jake, if she had the opportunity, as you say, why did she want him dead?"

"This is when it gets complicated. Buckle up, it's going to be quite a journey. Franny's brother, Elmo, was working on a real estate fraud with AJ and, for reasons I haven't yet figured out, Franny believed Kole would stop the scam in its tracks."

"Perhaps he threatened to go to the police?"

"Exactly. Kole was about to ruin everything and Franny wanted to make sure that her Elmo kept his piece of the action."

Sylvia nodded. As I described the case out loud, much of it made sense to me, as if for the first time.

"And on the night of the murder, where was AJ, and why did she confess to the crime?"

"There was a magic moment in the house that night. AJ and Kole argued over the dinner table. He stormed out of the room and AJ threw everything into the trash, plates and all. While the couple were separated, Franny came in, did away with Kole, and ran out again. The woman is nuts on a good day."

"And that was not her best evening."

"Not at all... Anyway, AJ comes back inside and maybe hears the commotion or wants to carry on the argument with Kole. She finds him dead and in a split second, she calls the police and admits to the murder so she can hide the fraud from the cops."

"Because she reckons if they sniff around too hard, even flatfeet from homicide will stop to check out piles of cash and real estate documents."

"Got it in one, Sylvia."

I sipped my coffee and allowed my grin to remain on my face as I basked in the glory of my tale. She sat and stared, deep in thought.

"Just one thing, Jake."

"What's that?"

"AJ paid you to find her guilty, not innocent."

"Technically, she gave me money so she could have her day in court."

"As a defendant, not as a witness for the prosecution."

"True. Perhaps the two women worked together to kill Kole and AJ didn't want the cops to look at Franny too closely."

"She is flighty."

"So now do you believe AJ created the argument with Kole and opened the door to Franny, who did the deed when AJ was outside with the trash?"

"Makes sense to me."

"Jake, if you ask me, this case rests on the testimony of AJ's neighbor."

"Gladys?"

"That's the one. Will you need stronger evidence to convince the DA?"

I sat there for a moment and the grin faded from my mouth. Sylvia was right. All I had was the word of a woman whose life was to stare out of windows and spread gossip about people.

"I must get more on Franny."

"Yes, you must, Jake."

She wandered over to the coffee pot.

"Want a top-up?"

I nodded, and she added two inches of java to each mug.

"Should you canvass the Langchamp area again?"

"The neighbors weren't much good the first time I interviewed them. I doubt if a couple of days have improved their memories."

"Jake, build up the case around Franny. If she's as flaky as you say, then she's bound to have slipped up somewhere along the way."

I did some calculations in my head and put down my coffee mug.

"Our drinks are going to have to take a rain check."

"Aw, shucks."

"I know. Maybe tomorrow instead. I need to spend the evening trying to position Franny in my crosshairs."

"Tomorrow then."

25

I LEFT SYLVIA to close up the office and headed over to the corner of West Palm and South Oleander Avenue. A good rule to follow when you are about to confront a killer is not to rush in before checking out the lie of the land. Those of us who survived Korea learned that the hard way.

So, instead of ringing the apartment buzzer, I loafed around the building and watched who came and left. That evening there was nobody to observe, but the idea was sound. I stepped back onto the opposite sidewalk and most of the lights were out. I focused my attention on where I figured Franny's place was located; either she was asleep or not at home.

The next best thing when about to hold a conversation with a murderer is to walk around a bit and see what information the neighborhood brings. This is a polite way of saying that I hunkered down by the building dumpster and hoped I wouldn't be forced to dive into that vast pool of unpleasantness.

"What are you doing, Mac?"

I swiveled round, my hand already on my piece, but the guy had both arms out, palms visible.

"Easy, fella. I didn't mean to startle you."

A building light behind me shone in his face. The man was in his forties, wearing a suit, and chewing a toothpick.

"What are you doing sneaking up on people like that?"

"The name's Joss Vipond and I could ask the same of you."

"Jake Adkins. I was just mooching around. What's your story?"

"I remember you were here earlier this week. You visited the Kennard place. And now you're snooping in the trash. Are you a private eye? I can't think of anyone else who'd behave the way you do; apart from a pervert."

"You're right first time."

I raised a hand so that Vipond did nothing stupid and pulled out my badge from my jacket pocket. He echoed my action and showed me his shield. He was a private dick too.

"What's your interest in this building, Joss?"

"Same as yours, it would appear."

"How's your investigation going?"

"Nice try, Jake, but I'm not about to reveal my client or my job so early in the conversation."

"A fella's got to ask."

"That's true. How long have you been monitoring the place?"

"Several days."

"Is it the building or an occupant that interests you?"

He grinned.

"An occupant."

"Is she in right now?"

"Yes," he grinned. "She's gone to sleep. The lights are off, if you haven't noticed."

I wondered if Vipond was right or if Franny had given him the slip. If I was correct and she had done for Kole, then she'd be smart enough to trick some PI into believing that she was in bed for the night.

"Listen, Jake. As we appear to share a mutual object of investigation, why don't we head off to a bar and carry on our conversation over a beer instead of standing next to a dumpster at the back of an apartment block?"

▬ ▬

JOSS LED A five-minute walk a couple of blocks, and we reached an Irish bar.

"Two beers, please."

The barkeep nodded before Joss placed the order.

"Been here before?"

"Once or twice."

When the drinks arrived, the barman popped them down.

"How's it going, Joss?"

"Not bad, Jeff."

"You must have had a memorable time for the staff to know who you are after only a couple of visits here."

He chewed his toothpick and smiled. Joss did a lot of that.

"Aw, maybe I've been here on a few more occasions than I said."

To keep him sweet, I grinned, but I couldn't understand why he felt the need to lie to me. If he was a barfly, I wouldn't judge. After all, this job can turn the strongest heart to mush within a couple of months. He looked as though he'd been at this game for much longer than that.

"How many days have you been on Kennard's tail, Jake?"

"Only this week. And you?"

"Started before the weekend."

"Are you investigating anything in particular, Joss?"

"Surveillance work only. I've a camera with a long lens and I'm paid for obtaining certain photos."

"Compromising ones?"

"Not like that. She's not playing under the sheets with anyone. Unless you tell me otherwise."

"I'm not aware of any action in that direction, Joss."

"Does that mean you're investigating her?"

"Not quite, but she has appeared as part of a line of inquiry on my case."

"Interesting."

We sipped our beers while Vipond pondered and I tried to figure out who was his client and why they wanted pictures of Franny.

"Tell me, Joss, if the photos weren't Franny in compromising positions, why were you taking them?"

"Apart from the money?" We both chuckled. "My client wished to know Franny's whereabouts, as you're asking, and the photos gave the proof of locations."

"Have you had to follow her around the city or has it been easy street?"

"Franny Kennard stays in her apartment most of the time, so yeah, I haven't had to spend too much on gas."

"Has she been anywhere unusual?"

"Not unless you think a trip to the grocery store is exciting."

"Is that the only place she's been?"

Joss put down his beer and stared at me.

"Not quite, Jake. I have photos of her in other locations."

"Oh?"

"Yes, Jake. Before you ask, I know every joint Franny's visited since I started the surveillance operations on Thursday last week."

He knew more than he was saying and I had yet to share my suspicions about my prime suspect in the Kole Kennard homicide.

"So that means you know where she was on, say, Saturday?"

"That's right."

"And how about Sunday?"

"Then too. I have photos of Kennard at every place she's been. No exceptions."

I swallowed hard.

"How about in the evening?"

"Every place she's been, Jake."

With those words, Joss got off his stool and swaggered over to the bathroom. The man knew about Sunday and if he had proof Franny was at the Langchamp residence, then he probably knew what happened when she was over there.

The guy sat back down and glugged the last remnants of his beer.

"Jeff, another round when you're ready."

The barman nodded at me and poured two more beers.

"Joss, could anyone view those photos?"

"Not just anybody, Jake. There would need to be some financial consideration. After all, you'd be asking me to break a client's confidentiality."

"That's between you and your paymaster. All I'm inquiring is if you could get me access to any film you took of Franny on Sunday evening if she was not at home. Was she in her apartment then?"

I'd thrown the sixty-four thousand dollar question over to Joss and waited for his response. He swigged a mouthful of beer.

"She was not."

"In that case, depending on the price, I may be interested in getting a copy of that film."

"I took two rolls that night."

"The only shots I want are of her at a particular residence. The rest are of no use to me."

"And where is this home?"

"South Fifth Plaza and East Ocean Boulevard."

He paused and considered matters for a moment. I wasn't sure if he was recalling whether Franny had been there or if he was selecting the bottom line for our monetary negotiation.

"I can confirm there are photos that you will find interesting."

"Spoken like a lawyer, Joss, but we need to discuss your fee. How much do you want?"

"Five hundred."

I almost snorted a mouthful of beer out of my nose.

"You've got me mistaken for another guy. That's more than I'm getting for a week's work. You have my total respect if that's what you charge for a couple of black-and-whites."

"They're in color."

"Even so, Joss. This is coming out of my end, not from my client, and I need to pay the rent and put food on the table."

"Two C notes?"

I liked a man who could pivot on a dime.

"And then I have staff bills to cover."

"One hundred?"

"And gas in my car. I've already had to drive out to Malibu for no good reason."

"Fifty?"

I held out my hand, and we shook. The art of financial negotiation is to never mention a number. I'd learned that from Ed, but no one had coached Joss over the years.

"You get the photos and I'll find your money. Let's meet up in an hour."

He gave me the address of his office. We knocked back our drinks and departed into the night.

26

JOSS VIPOND'S OFFICE was half a mile from mine on the fifth floor of a serviced building. Judging by the state of the paintwork, my rent was at least going on the upkeep of the joint. I reminded myself not to complain the next time the landlord renegotiated the lease.

I found the place with no problem and sauntered past the empty reception desk on the first floor. Up in the elevator and Joss's office was the fourth on the right. A janitor mopped the floor as I wandered by.

A light shone behind the frosted glass of the door, so I knocked and entered. I wasn't surprised to find myself standing in front of a receptionist's desk occupied by a pretty secretary. She must have been paid double time, given the hour of the night. The chances were she hadn't been doing anything interesting anyway, like having drinks with her boss.

"Jake Adkins, and I'm here to see Joss."

She wrote my name on her pad and took it and herself into an adjoining room. Ten seconds later she appeared and held the door open for me.

"You may see Mr. Vipond now."

Joss relaxed in a large armchair, which reminded me of my own inner sanctum. I looked warily at the client's seating, which didn't appear as inviting. I sat down and the chair's wooden frame creaked as it tried to absorb my one-hundred-and-fifty pounds.

"You got the photos?"

"Yep."

He tapped his desk, and I assumed he wanted to imply they were in a drawer. For an instant, I considered rushing him and grabbing the prints without due payment, but then I slapped myself back to sense. We both had guns and vast experience in difficult situations. The chances were he was training his piece on me as we spoke. That's what I would do if I were sprawled in the swivel chair.

"Jake, did you bring the cash?"

I patted my jacket to indicate that there was green for him, although I always kept money in my pants pocket. Gesturing toward my lap felt inappropriate under the circumstances.

"Before we exchange goods for monies, Joss, no disrespect, but how can I be certain that the pictures you're offering me were taken on the night in question?"

"What do you expect, Jake? The day's newspaper in the corner of every shot?"

"It would help."

He was unimpressed with my quip, but he had a point. I wasn't sure what I needed for proof, but I knew Joss's word on the stand might not be enough, even if a DA could convince him to talk. The man could hide behind client confidentiality without batting an eyelid.

"You're going to have to trust me on this one, Jake."

"Joss, don't get me wrong, I'm fine with this, but if the matter ends up in a courtroom, I need to know that the information you provide is sound."

"I'll refuse to name my client, but for an appropriate fee, I will take the stand and confirm the location of the photos."

That was as good as it was going to get. The promise of corroborating evidence from a third party was more than I could have hoped. I pulled out the green from my pocket and Joss took an envelope from his top drawer.

He pushed it forward across his desk, keeping his palm on top. I placed the money down as well and shoved it away from me by a few inches. We eyed each other up, weighing how much we could trust each other. I decided this was getting stupid.

"Let's stop horsing around."

I let go of the notes and pounced on the envelope. Joss did the same in reverse and we both pulled back our respective bounty. He counted the singles I had provided, and I opened the letter to see what I had bought.

There was a solitary photo inside and I yanked it out into the light. I hadn't left the room and already I felt stiffed by the cockroach; our deal had been for the purchase of photographs plural. I recognized the Langchamp interior and what looked like the master bedroom. Although it was out of focus, there appeared to be a body on the floor. The clearest thing was Franny, front and center, walking away from the corpse.

"You must have been in the backyard tree when you took this."

"I reckon I was."

"And you saw everything through your camera lens?"

"Uh-huh."

"Are there any other shots taken before this one of Franny in the room?"

"Only of her back. You can't identify her from them."

"Any of her committing the murder?"

"No. I watched more than I photographed. Most of the time, I was trying to work out what she was doing there, and I didn't expect her to do what she did."

"How long did you stay in that tree afterward?"

"A minute. No more. The last thing I wanted was to be found up there when the cops came stomping through."

"Did you call them?"

"I was up in the darn tree."

"Later, when you'd left the area."

"Now why would I drop a dime informing those fine police detectives of a murder I had witnessed if I wasn't going to hang around and help them with their investigation?"

"Civic duty? You had just seen a murder."

"I wasn't being paid to assist the cops. I was employed to take the pictures."

"And who did you say paid you, Joss?"

"I never did and I ain't starting now either. That fact will go with me to my grave."

I stared at the photograph again and tried to decide if there really was a body on show in the background. Perhaps it was only a shadow or a bag on the floor. I squinted and drew the picture nearer hoping I'd see things more clearly, but it didn't work.

In my hand was a fuzzy photo of Franny walking away from what Vipond would testify was a murder, but only if he was paid. Not the greatest night's work in my life, but quite profitable, nonetheless. If you ignore the fact it cost me fifty bucks.

Perhaps he could sense my disquiet because Joss rummaged around in his drawers and popped a second photo onto his desk.

"You can have this one too if you like. No charge."

I picked it up. This must have been taken a few seconds later because Franny stood right by the bedroom door. It was just as out of focus as the other picture, but at least he had kept his end of the deal in terms of the number of photos in my possession. I thanked him and got up to shake hands.

SAT IN MY car, I took out both photos from the envelope to stare at them again. I wondered who would pay a private eye to follow Franny. The surveillance dated back to at least the previous week, and this photo might well depict Kole's murder. Or rather, its immediate aftermath.

What it didn't show was anybody killing anyone else and we would still need to rely on Joss's testimony to place Franny at the scene and as the hand that committed the crime.

Although it wasn't perfect, the more I looked at the images, the more convinced I became Franny had done the deed. Vipond wasn't the most trustworthy soul, but he had been following Miss Kennard and had no reason to accuse her without justification. And there was Franny's letter threatening the guy.

I had means, opportunity in a photograph, and motive. All I needed to do now to tie this up in a pretty bow was to confront her and get a confession before I called Lou and dragged him out of his bed.

The good news was that I knew where she was. Joss had told me the woman had gone to sleep before I arrived at her apartment. So I popped the pictures in the envelope and drove back over to Franny's place.

27

I PARKED OUTSIDE the apartment building; there was no need to hide my arrival. As I stepped out of the car, I heard the rustle of leaves and wondered whether Joss had followed me and was taking photos from the undergrowth. No matter.

Fewer lights than earlier were on because some of the night owls in the block had gone to sleep. In contrast, Franny's light was now on, so she might have popped out while Joss and I conducted our business.

Or she woke up and was in the kitchen having a cookie and a glass of milk. At least I wouldn't have the hassle of banging on the door to get her out of bed. That involved annoying all the neighbors before the person opened up and let me in.

Given I knew she was awake, I pressed the buzzer to be let in, but there was no reply. I tried again. Nothing.

The chances of me tailgating a resident at this point in the night were slender to none, so I whipped out Old Faithful and wiggled the bolt until the mechanism sprang open.

Some people devote time to picking the lock itself, but I only do that if my first method proves unhelpful. Most bolts yield within seconds because they are poorly made and badly fitted.

Once in the lobby, I made my way to Franny's apartment and stopped. My initial impulse was to tap on the door hoping Franny would respond, but without waking the neighbors. No luck.

Rat-a-tat-tat. A proper noise, generated by my knuckles and not my fingertips. I waited, but still nothing. Leaning against the door, I tried to listen for signs of activity. She might have fallen asleep before switching off her light, overcome by tiredness and cookies.

As my ear pressed against the entranceway, it moved an inch; the door was ajar. This is never a good sign in the middle of the night and I drew my gun. I inched my weary hide into the hallway and halted. No sounds. Aware there may be an intruder in the place, I refrained from calling out to let Franny know I was in her home.

Instead, with my revolver pointing forward, I edged toward the living room. I peeked around the corner and found… an empty room. I exhaled.

All the doors were shut, so I padded over to the kitchen and examined the crack surrounding the jamb. It didn't seem as though a light was on, so I opened the door with one hand while maintaining the position of my piece in front of me. Just in case.

But all that greeted me on the other side was a dark cooking space. Back to the living room and I faced a choice between trying the bathroom or Franny's bedroom. I flipped a coin in my head and her boudoir won. The door wasn't completely shut, so I pushed it a little with one finger to get a better view. I saw an empty bed, which hadn't been slept in. So much for my milk and cookies theory.

Perhaps Joss wasn't such a great surveillance operative and Franny had given him the slip earlier on, only to return while he and I were not at our station. Just to make sure she wasn't hiding behind the door thinking that I was a burglar, I walked into the room. She didn't jump out at me because she wasn't there.

Somebody had switched on the bedroom and living room lights and it was not me. I wandered back to check out the only room left. When I opened the bathroom door, I found Franny hanging from the ceiling light fitting. Whoever had installed it had done a better job than the cowboys who put in the main entrance locks.

⸺ ⸺

NOW FRANNY HAD placed me in a difficult position. The option most would choose would have been to rush to the phone and call the police, but that was not my first instinct.

As soon as that happened, there would be a slew of questions aimed at me and what I was doing in the apartment at that time of night, how I knew Franny, and did I know anyone who might want to cause her harm, as well as a firm but polite request for an alibi.

Another option was to stand still and do nothing. That was what I did. If she had killed Kole, and I had the evidence to indicate that she did, then perhaps she did herself in with the remorse of it all.

She was highly strung and that might have been her response to the tragic situation. Why would she have waited so long to do it, though? I had no answer to that.

The other possibility was that this was not a suicide, but a murder. My mind raced, thinking of all the people who might want Franny Kennard dead.

Perhaps Elmo had discovered what his sister had done and was so enraged that he hanged her? Not so much a crime of passion as a crime of malice. And it was a cold way to kill his sibling. An icy method to do away with anybody.

Had Joss murdered her at the behest of his mystery client and used me as an elaborate alibi? That was worth a second consideration. I felt like a patsy standing in the living room, careful not to touch anything in case the cops found my fingerprints later that night. I looked down and noticed a half-inch square patch of damp on the floor, but paid no more attention to it.

AJ was the only other person who knew Franny that I was aware of. Maybe this was a revenge attack for killing Kole. If so, it was pretty dumb because she was such an obvious suspect. And she was smarter than that. AJ had been educated in France, after all.

As little as I thought of Vipond, I doubted whether he had snuck back here, killed Franny, and then escaped in the time it took me to get to the apartment. Or he could have swung by here after leaving the bar and meeting me in his office later. Either possibility would have been a heroic trip and Joss didn't come across as capable of operating at that kind of level.

Suicide was the only solution.

THIS LEFT ME with only one item on my to-do list. It was time to let the cops know there was another corpse in LA County. I direct-dialed into the precinct and asked for Inspector Lou Granger. The receptionist put me on hold and I waited while they found my old friend and he swallowed the remains of his donut.

"Hello?"

"It's Jake here."

"Shouldn't you be tucked up in bed at this hour?"

"I'm about to go to sleep, but consider it my civic duty to pass on some information to you flatfoots before I slip into the land of nod."

He sighed; a blast of air hit the receiver and slammed into my ear.

"What do you want to get off your chest, Jake? I've told you before that you have an alibi for the murder of Abe Lincoln."

"This isn't anything I've done, Lou."

I changed the tone of my voice to something more somber and, being an intelligent inspector, he picked up on my cue.

"Who's dead, Jake?"

"What makes you believe there has to be a homicide?"

"You've called me in the middle of the night and you only do that when there's a corpse."

He was right. I must stop doing this.

"Got it in one. I doubt if it was murder, Lou, but there is a dead body and I couldn't think of anyone else who deserved to hear the news first."

"Are you beside it now?"

"No, but I found out only a moment or two ago."

Every word I said was the truth, as I never counted lying by omission.

"Besides, I told you I was about to go to bed. And before you ask, no, there isn't a corpse resting next to me."

"With you, anything is possible."

"I didn't realize you held me in such low esteem."

"I'm joshing with you. Pay no never mind. Where's the body?"

I gave him the address in which I stood.

"Do you know who it is?"

"Franny Kennard. She's the sister of Elmo Kennard, who was involved with Kole and AJ Langchamp."

I paused, waiting for the volcano to explode. Three, two, one.

"What the hell have you got yourself involved in, Jake? And what the hell had Franny Kennard got to do with the death of Kole Langchamp?"

"I'm not sure how much I can tell you, Lou. My hands are tied by client privilege. There's not much else that I can tell you."

"I'll be the judge, and there's a lot more explanation that needs to come out of your mouth."

The best plan was to say nothing because Lou was not in the mood.

"If you are in bed, how did you learn of the suicide?"

"I'll tell you some other time. Right now, pay a visit to the apartment. You have a corpse to deal with."

The sound of a grown man growling down the phone was the last thing I heard, as I thought it best to end the call and leave the building.

THURSDAY

28

IF I HAD gone back to my apartment, then I knew Lou would come knocking and as much as I liked the guy, I didn't want to answer any of his questions. So I did the only honorable thing and hid in a motel and fell asleep.

That morning, I phoned Sylvia and asked her to bring my spare suit over to my hideaway, because even though I was less tired, I still had no desire to be interrogated by Lou or one of his henchmen.

She took one look at my accommodation and left. The offer of breakfast was insufficient to keep her in the vicinity. Sylvia was right; I had found a fleapit and exited the place as soon as I could put on my pants.

I ate at a nearby diner and used the time for my toast and juice to arrive to ponder over the previous night.

Franny killed Kole out of a jealousy born from wanting to protect her brother and then, in a sinkhole of remorse, woke up and hanged herself. That was the sum of it. AJ wanted rid of Kole too and gave Franny the opportunity to do the deed. AJ covered for the sister by confessing to the police that it was all her doing so the cops wouldn't find out about the real estate scam she had going on with Jack Dragna's land.

For me to get AJ her day in court, I would need to tread carefully with Lou, but also I needed to speak with Elmo again. When we first met, I didn't know the right questions to ask, and he wasn't that forthcoming, anyway. Eager to please, but not keen to inform.

With Elmo's sister now deceased, the police would come knocking to tell him of Franny's fate any minute now. I needed to get to him first before he was whisked away to identify her body and fill out the paperwork.

I hightailed it over to Elmo's place and entered the building when a neighbor walked out for their morning promenade. Up to the third floor to find his apartment door ajar. I swallowed hard and dreaded the possibility that both siblings had killed themselves on the same night. That would have been more than a coincidence.

I needn't have worried because I discovered Elmo in his living room, face down in a pool of blood. You'd need the best defense attorney in the country to convince a jury that this was a suicide.

———

I SIGHED AND holstered my pistol. The Kennard family was not having a good day. Careful not to get blood on my clothes, or leave an incriminating fingerprint in the red mess, I placed two fingers on his jugular to make sure there was no need to phone for an ambulance. Nada.

Then I looked around near the body to see if there was anything interesting. There was no sign of blood pooling on his back, so I assumed the slug was still inside him and that I would not find it lodged in a wall. But I searched for one anyway. No joy.

Under ordinary circumstances, I would have gone through each room and checked out every hole for evidence. Only these were extraordinary times, and the cops would arrive any minute to interview the corpse over Franny's death.

A thought shot across my mind like a bolt of lightning. What if Franny had killed Elmo and then hanged herself in remorse? Her suicide would make a lot more sense; plug him in the middle of the night and return home racked with guilt.

That begged the question of why she wanted to kill him when the reason for murdering Kole was to give her brother the happiness he deserved. Sometimes you don't have all the answers when standing next to a corpse.

I shoved my hand down the back of every drawer I could find, as that is where amateurs try to hide objects from professionals. Apart from some splinters in my wrists, I had nothing to show for the experience. Then I hopped into the bedroom and searched under the mattress, another childish hiding place. Bupkis.

Next, I tried my favorite location: the trashcan in the kitchen. The good news was that there were no recent food deposits. However, the bad news was that I found nothing of interest either. The man had no incriminating paperwork that I could see and in my head, sirens wailed as Lou rushed over to catch me red-handed with Elmo's bloody corpse.

I blinked and attempted to imagine where Elmo might have kept his private papers. They must be somewhere, if only I could figure out where they were hidden.

Another idea flitted into my brain. What if Joss had lied and Elmo had killed Kole? In this scenario, AJ will have lied to protect her business partner, who may also have been her lover.

Franny finds out all about them when she witnesses Kole's murder. She is so distraught that a couple of days later, she has it out with her brother. She shoots him and, filled with remorse, hangs herself as soon as she returns to her apartment. AJ again lies to hide the real estate scam from the police.

Not impossible, but I had no evidence to tie any of these possibilities to reality. Lou would not be impressed with any of these suggestions because they were all circumstantial. My ears pricked up as I thought I discerned a siren in the distance.

Now was not the time to be caught standing next to a fresh corpse. I might not have found any evidence I could use to prove AJ should be put on trial, but I had discovered another dead body and even Lou wouldn't be able to shrug that off as a harmless coincidence.

There was definitely a siren approaching, and I figured a neighbor must have dropped a dime. I peeped out of the window that looked onto the street. A police car was pulling up outside the block. Without waiting to see if the officers were responding to a domestic dispute next door or the murder in Elmo's home in which I was crouching, I ran out of the apartment and hit the stairs. No flatfoot would want to waste shoe leather when there was an elevator to take the strain.

Sure enough, as I got to the stairwell, the mechanics of the elevator shifted and groaned as the cops stood in the tiny box and waited for it to arrive on the third floor.

Meanwhile, I raced down the stairs, making record time to reach the first floor. I lingered and listened, pressed against the wall before I opened the door, and marched through the now-empty reception area, out of the entrance, and straight to my car, keeping my eyes hidden by my fedora.

Once the cops found Elmo's body, I knew it was only a matter of time before Lou would come calling. The man was my friend, but he was also a detective and two Kennards dead in less than twenty-four hours, both of whom were known to my client was the sort of situation that he would be expected to investigate quite closely.

The best thing I could do was head to my inner sanctum and wait for the storm to come knocking.

29

TWENTY MINUTES AFTER I put my feet up on my desk and rifled through the newspaper Sylvia had brought in for me, she told me there was a call for me.

"What the hell have you been up to, Jake?"

"Hi, Lou. Did you get to the bottom of the Franny Kennard affair?"

"Don't talk to me as though I'm an idiot. What have you got messed up in?"

"I don't know what you're talking about. Sounds like there's trouble. Can I help?"

If I didn't know better, I would swear Lou's molars ground away.

"Jake, of all the people in the world who might try to pretend to be innocent, you are the last one on the planet I'd believe."

"There's no need to be like that, Lou."

"Isn't there? The only reason you're not sitting in handcuffs is because we go back a ways. You'd better come over to Elmo Kennard's place and explain yourself."

"Tell me the address and I'll be happy to pop over."

"I'm no fool. We both know you've been here before."

"You're at Elmo's apartment now?"

"Uh-huh. And it's a crime scene, as you surely are aware."

"What's happened?"

"Don't give me that. You get your ass over here this minute or I will put out an all-points and you can be grabbed by some greenhorn in uniform."

"I'll be right over, Lou."

* * *

WHEN I ARRIVED at the block, there were flashing lights everywhere. Two squad cars and Lou's beat-up saloon. Perhaps he was the guy who tried to knock me off the sidewalk. He had every right, given how much I messed him about over the years. That said, there's been more than one case I solved for which he took full credit. Just saying.

The uniform who stood at the police tape to prevent civilians from wandering into the crime scene refused to allow me entry at first. Then I dropped my name and he allowed me through. Into the elevator and down the corridor toward Elmo's place. It was teeming with cops, coming and going with a uniformed officer standing outside the apartment door.

As I approached, a voice from inside barked, "Let the louse in." I strode into the living room and tipped my hat to Lou, who glared at me and pointed at the floor.

"What do you know about that?"

The cops had covered Elmo with a sheet, but the edges of the pool of blood that had formed around his body were still visible.

"He's dead."

"Now tell me something I don't know."

"There's not much I can say, Lou. I'm being paid by a client and what I know is protected by client privilege."

"Have you fired your gun recently?"

My jaw dropped. Lou had never accused me of murder before.

"No. Check if you want."

I held my jacket open with my left hand and removed my piece from its holster. Lou grabbed it and looked in the chamber. All the bullets were present and correct. Then he took my sleeve and stared at the end. He was looking for gunshot residue on my fingers and wrist. There was nothing to find, but that didn't placate him.

"Do you know who did for Kennard?"

"No, I don't, and if I did, then I couldn't tell you, Lou. Have you boys narrowed down a time of death?"

"Lowbridge will only say sometime between nine last night and three in the morning until he gets the body back for a postmortem."

"Any idea if he was killed before or after Franny committed suicide?"

He shook his head.

"With all the client privilege you're hiding behind, I reckon you might have gathered some facts along the way. As always, you are just a bundle of guesses and hypotheticals."

"That's me, Lou. I know nothing, and I say even less."

He snorted at me.

"Lou, you didn't answer my question. Who died first?"

"Your guess is as good as mine. Lowbridge hasn't examined the other Kennard yet, so we must both wait."

"Spencer never rushes, does he?"

"Nope. That's because his patients aren't in the habit of running away."

"I heard that."

Spencer Lowbridge appeared as if from nowhere and busied himself with the body. Lou and I smiled and moved into the hallway to allow the medical examiner to continue to do his job in peace.

"Jake, I'm going to need you to come with me to the station house."

"My car's outside. Is it all right if I follow you in it?"

"A uniform must stay with you. It's nothing personal, but you're the only link between the two Kennard deaths and you knew about at least one before I did. That makes you a person of interest at best."

＊＊＊

WHEN I ARRIVED at the precinct, the flatfoot took me to an interview room and dumped me there for an eternity. I understood how these things played out and did my best not to wave at whoever was staring at me through the two-way mirror. After I had been sitting there for fifteen minutes, I reckoned Lou was watching while believing he was making me sweat.

A moment later, he burst into the room and sat down opposite me. He offered me a smoke, which I accepted.

"I'm not under arrest, Lou, am I?"

"Inspector Granger to you. And not at present."

"My apologies. No disrespect was intended."

I played to the gallery, as I didn't want Lou to get into any trouble for consorting with alleged witnesses.

"Do you know who killed Elmo Kennard?"

"Inspector, I haven't got a clue."

"And what about Franny Kennard?"

"I thought she was a suicide."

"Did you discover the body?

"I have been working a case for a client and the information I possess is privileged."

This time, I sure heard Lou grind his molars. I felt his predicament. He understood I had something to tell him, but he knew he'd need a judge to force me to say it out loud. Worse for him was that he knew me well enough to know that I'd take a few nights in a cell for contempt, rather than spill my guts about a client's business.

"Did you kill Elmo Kennard?"

"No, of course not. Why would I want to do something as stupid as that?"

He had no answer and after dancing around the issue for another thirty minutes, he threw me in a holding cell anyway. I reckoned he wanted to punish me for not helping him to do his job some more. By the time this was all over, I planned to get the DA to take on AJ's case, as well as put Elmo's murder to bed.

I might not have had all the pieces to play with, but every ounce of information I had in my possession connected somehow.

When they let me out, I decided not to push my luck and offer Lou a drink at O'Malley's. Instead, I went home to change. I'd spent less than an hour in the cells, but I felt dirty.

WITH A FRESHLY laundered shirt, I skipped back to the office where Sylvia sat, awaiting any visitors.

"I put the post on your newspaper so you wouldn't miss it."

"Thanks. Anything interesting?"

"Two bills and a white handwritten envelope."

"Sounds intriguing."

"I'll make you a coffee."

I hustled to my desk and focused on the letter. Even when I held it up to the light, I couldn't see inside. This was good quality stationery. I ripped it open and unfolded a letter, written with intense, spidery handwriting.

Jake

Kole Langchamp is dead and so is Elmo.

I need you to know that I had nothing to do with either of their sad endings.

But my world is closing in on me and I must go now.

Franny Kennard

Another quick glance at the envelope and I checked there was a stamp, so it had been through the postal service, but the timeline was screwed up. Was there a mailbox in LA that enabled you to throw a letter into it at night and get the post delivered the next morning?

Franny might have taken it to Central Avenue and dropped it off there. I held the corner with the stamp up close and squinted. There might have been a postmark, but I was not certain.

My natural inability to believe what was in front of my nose made me wonder who could have sent the letter if it wasn't Franny. And why would someone want me to believe that Elmo's sister had nothing to do with the death of Kole Langchamp?

30

SYLVIA KNOCKED AND entered the inner sanctum, carrying a steaming mug of coffee for me. She sat down with her notepad on her lap.

"If we can't have a drink after hours, the least I can do is get you a java in the office."

"Thanks, Sylvia, and sorry about last night. Duty calls: you know the drill. With a bit of luck, we shall grab a martini tonight instead. If you're free, that is."

"For you, Jake. Any time."

The corner of her mouth curled up, but she chose not to allow a full smile to form. Cute girl.

"What happened after Lou bawled you out?"

"When you listen on the line, you should at least pretend that you were busy doing something else."

"Where would the fun be in that, Jake? It's not like I share the conversations with anybody else."

Curves in all the right places and a brain between her ears. What more could a man desire?

"Everyone is dying on me, Sylvia. This is my problem. First Franny and now Elmo."

"A family curse?"

"The only person I know who connects them is AJ, but why would she murder her business partner, let alone a crazy woman like Franny? Nobody listened to her, not when she was alive at any rate."

"What do you mean?"

I handed over the letter for Sylvia to read.

"Shouldn't you give this to Lou?"

"I will in time. Right now, I need to figure out whether it's real."

She held the paper up to the light to check the watermark.

"Seems like an original to me."

"I meant I want to know if Franny wrote it."

"Why don't you compare her handwriting?"

"The letter she sent to AJ was typed. I've only got her signature on that. Besides, this was produced by a frenetic hand; to type a note to threaten somebody's death is cold. It took a level of planning that this scrawl does not offer."

Sylvia dropped the missive back on my desk.

"The biggest problem is the sheer lack of hard evidence. There's Joss's photograph and two letters which might have been sent by Franny."

"Don't forget Julius Warner. Do you reckon AJ is a…" She leaned forward and lowered her voice. "…a bigamist."

"Or a Mormon," I replied with a straight face, but I didn't believe my own words.

"When she was in the office, she never came over all godly."

"I'm joking, Sylvia."

Her cheeks reddened, and she covered her mouth with her fingers.

"You shouldn't mess with a simple country girl."

"I'm sorry, but you must be used to me by now."

"Just when you believe you know a person…"

"Aw, don't be like that. I'll make it up to you when we go out for cocktails. Choose the swankiest bar in town if you want."

Her eyes lit up.

"Really?"

"Would I lie to you?"

"That's the problem with you, Jake. Half the time, I just don't know."

"Never about anything important."

We fell silent for a spell, each captured by our own thoughts.

"Three dead bodies, one confession that the DA doesn't believe, and bupkis beyond that."

"It's not looking good, Jake. Will AJ ask for her money back?"

"If I don't convince the district attorney to put her on trial, then she might well try. But there was no condition of success on the paper I got her to sign on Monday."

"Spoken like a true lawyer."

I glanced at my lap.

"I'm surrounded by corpses, Sylvia."

"You'll figure it out. You always do."

"I usually do. This is a strange case, though. I should never have taken it on. Next time a client comes in here protesting their guilt, slap me and tell me to send them on their way."

"Are you eating properly? You look gray and all washed up."

I shrugged. Coffee and cake had been the principal food of choice since AJ walked into my life, but I recalled chomping on a steak at some point this week.

"Why don't I drive you back to your place and fix you something to eat? A square meal will only help you think straight."

In the absence of any better ideas, I agreed to Sylvia's suggestion.

SYLVIA WAS A careful driver in the main, but every so often, she'd swerve into another lane, as though instructed by an inner demon. I gripped my seat and pretended not to be in fear for my life. The girl was doing her best for me.

At the apartment, she hurried into the kitchen and I headed to the bedroom and sat on the edge of the bed. Her humming wafted around my apartment. She must have quite a pair of lungs to be loud enough for me to hear her through two sets of doors and as many walls. Perhaps she was in a choir. I made a mental note to ask her.

I hopped in the en suite shower and then dried myself down. I wrapped the towel around my waist as I stood in front of my wardrobe to decide which of my white shirts and black suits I should change into.

Just before I stepped into my shorts, I considered the notion that Sylvia had taken me home, told me to get undressed, and then made me lunch. In almost any other situation, I'd expect to find her curled up on my bed when I left the bathroom.

She was cut from a different cloth. I got dressed and sauntered to the kitchen, where Sylvia stood with a frying pan in one hand.

"Don't just stand there gawping. Do something useful and lay the table."

I did as instructed and a few minutes later, we sat down together and she placed a steak on my plate and shoveled a load of vegetables by its side.

"Boy, that smells good."

"Thank you very much."

"Aren't you going to eat anything?"

"Silly me."

Sylvia stood back up and poured some veg on her plate.

"No steak for you?"

"I've got to watch my figure."

"Leave that to other people. You look peachy to me."

She slapped me on the arm to dismiss my statement and sprinkled salt over her food. That was something I got out of the habit of using because of my tour in Korea. Condiments are a luxury when the enemy is sending bullets to whizz past your ear and you don't know if you will ever eat again.

We chowed down in silence, but after this amount of time, we were comfortable enough in each other's company not to feel the need to fill the void with small talk. Afterward, I washed up while she watched and I put on a pot of coffee. When it was brewed, I placed a pair of mugs on the table and returned to my seat.

"Three bodies, Sylvia."

"The first and third you know are murder; it's only Franny that might be a suicide."

"Sure."

"And if we have two more murders on our hands, in addition to Kole Langchamp, that is, then the chances are that you are looking for one culprit."

"That makes sense, but only if we ignore what we know. Franny was seen at the Langchamp residence on the night of Kole's murder, but AJ says it was her. Franny appears to have died by her own hand and I might have evidence where she denies killing Kole. Then we have Elmo in deep with AJ, but shot from close range."

"How do you know that?"

"The blood splatter. It was tight around the body, so a high, intense impact rather than a defuse slug fired from across the room."

Sylvia turned up her nose.

"Sorry, but you asked."

"There are some things about this line of work that I will always detest."

"It's a grubby job, but someone has to do it."

She smiled, pretending to agree with me, but I could tell in her eyes that she reckoned the police would get by just fine without me. And at this point in the day, I think she might have been right.

"What are you going to do about the lack of evidence?"

"There is one man I know who will have scoured both scenes and found a mound of clues."

"Is this the same man who stuck you in a cell to shut you up for a while?"

"The selfsame fella. He might not want to see me, but I must pay Lou a visit."

31

THIS TIME WHEN I walked into the precinct, there was a palpable silence in the building, as though everyone knew why I was there and Lou had warned them about me. My footsteps echoed on the tiled floor as I approached the desk sergeant.

"I'm here to see Inspector Granger."

"And who wishes to speak with him?"

"Jake Adkins."

If I didn't know better, I'd swear an eyebrow rose before the flatfoot rang through to Lou. A smile after the conversation ended.

"He says for you to go to hell, but be in the usual place in twenty minutes."

I thanked the flatfoot and sauntered out of the building, knowing I had ample time to make a journey that was a matter of a few hundred feet. By the time Lou arrived, I was halfway through my first beer.

"What can I get you, Lou?"

"Some peace and quiet, and God's honest truth."

I smirked and ordered the inspector a beer.

"Get me a whiskey chaser too."

The barman delivered the drinks to the counter, and we clinked glasses.

"Lou, I need your help."

"And why should I do that? You've been stomping all over my crime scenes night and day, and bodies are piling up around you. Some in the precinct house reckon I should arrest you on suspicion of committing a double homicide."

"Do you believe them?"

"Forget about the war, but I reckon over the years you've murdered two people, just not the Kennard family."

"Gee, I'll take that as a compliment."

"Do whatever you want, Jake. You're holding back on me and I've got cases to close."

"We both agree AJ killed Kole Langchamp."

"Yes, the DA says voluntary manslaughter and you claim second-degree homicide. But those are minor details in the grand scheme of things right now."

"Lou, I've been thinking. I need to put my cards on the table."

"I knew an hour in a cell would get you in a more helpful frame of mind."

"Not really. I had a decent meal prepared by an attractive woman. That cleared my head."

My friend smiled at me.

"Are you going to introduce me?"

"Sometime, for sure, but she's not important this minute."

"You want to wait for a second date. I understand."

"Technically, we haven't had a first one yet, but that's another story."

"You always were a fast mover, Jake. I have to hand it to you. Who else would get a girl to cook for him before he's slept with her?"

"Forget about my meal, Lou. As far as I am aware, she may have killed Kole, but there is no reason for AJ to have murdered Franny and Elmo…"

"Uh-huh."

"Which means there is a second killer on the loose. If it's not me and it's not you, then who?"

Lou sipped his beer.

"Who are our suspects?"

"Now we arrive at my problem. I'm not certain there's anybody left to investigate."

"Do you believe a stranger did them in?"

"We both know that's unlikely. Someone is the link between the death of the siblings."

"How are you so sure Franny didn't kill Elmo and then hang herself?"

"Because she told me so."

Lou almost spat out his beer.

"I received a letter from what appears to be her where she denies killing her brother."

I pulled the letter out of my jacket and let Lou read it. He attempted to grab it from me, but I pulled it beyond his grasp.

"If anyone from the private eye union knew I'd even shown you this, I would be drummed out of the club. I want you to know this exists, but I can't give it over to you. Not until the case I'm being paid to sort out gets closed."

"Is this your idea of blackmail? You'll hand it over to me in exchange for the DA prosecuting Avril Langchamp?"

"That's not what I meant, but it sounds a great deal to me."

I winked at him.

"Let me think about it. If your client pleads guilty without wasting court time, then the district attorney might go for a suspended sentence."

"Now there's something to consider, Lou. In the meantime, you look but do not touch."

"You sound like my first wife."

"We'd agreed never to mention that woman to each other ever again."

"Shared history, Jake. You can't escape it."

"But I do try to forget."

I ordered another whiskey chaser each and downed mine fast, in memory of Lou's wife, who left us both. If you didn't know me better, you'd believe I spent my life going out with other fella's wives, but, at that point, it had only happened with Veronica and Mae.

We got lost in our memories for a while but then circled back to the three corpses.

"Do you reckon Franny wrote the note?"

"I'm not sure, Lou. She was not secure in herself. From what her neighbors said to me, she'd go crazy one moment and obsessive the next. The handwriting speaks volumes about somebody's state of mind, but do I know for certain this is hers? I don't have the faintest idea."

"If not Franny, then who and why?"

"Lou, I've been asking myself that since it landed on my desk this morning. The murderer could have sent it as a double bluff."

"You believe this master criminal posted a note from Franny that we won't believe came from her, so we'd think it was from somebody else. And then we dismiss the idea because it is too far-fetched."

"Now you say it out loud, it sounds stupid."

"You reckon?"

My cheeks heated up, and I sipped my beer because the back of my throat was dry.

"Firing into Elmo's chest made that a deliberate act, right?"

"Jake, you know it was not phoning the police that tells us it was intentional. There might have been an argument between Kennard and our unknown assailant. A finger is placed on the trigger. A twitch and the gun goes off by accident. All that is possible, but when she flees the scene, it's a sign of guilt."

"A woman? Where'd that come from?"

"Me and the boys back at the precinct have a working theory."

"And what is that?"

"None of these deaths required much physical force, which means it might be a woman."

"Are you counting Franny as a murder then?"

"I have an open mind on that one. But the circumstances of Kole's death and a bullet in Elmo's chest; even a petite woman could have carried out both those acts."

"Have the boys come up with any other leads or evidence?"

"Not yet. We've still got the Elmo Kennard apartment to finish looking through. If we're lucky, we'll discover a fingerprint we can use. I hope you remembered to wear gloves."

"Don't get smart with me, Lou Granger. You won't find my prints there for one simple reason."

"I know, you weren't there."

"Close. I didn't touch anything."

Another wink from me and Lou chuckled. We both knew what I'd done, but my friend had the decency not to accuse me of anything he'd need to arrest me over.

"Was there anything in Franny's apartment your forensic boffins found?"

"No fingerprints. Nothing incriminating to connect her to Kole's death. And even less to join the dots between Elmo and her, if you ignore the obvious fact they were related by blood."

As we finished our beers, we talked about baseball and women, like friends do. When his glass was finished, Lou wiped his upper lip on his sleeve, thanked me for the drinks, and returned to the precinct house.

I decided not to tell him about Julius Warner. His absence didn't put my client in a good light, and all I had was an empty trailer and a marriage certificate with AJ's name on it. My thinking was simple. The guy was in the wind and there were two dead bodies unaccounted for.

He was the only piece of the jigsaw puzzle that didn't fit until the Kennards became extinct. Then he looked like the exact right shape for the murderer. Why withhold that from Lou? Because I couldn't be sure AJ wasn't tied into all this.

Besides, it was my duty not to hand her over to the police. She might be paying me to ensure she had her day in court, but the intention was for her to be found not guilty of murder; fraud was not meant to be on the indictment sheet.

32

ALL THE EVENTS this week began with Kole Langchamp's murder, so I went back to the source and started again. Gladys Blake was the person who witnessed Franny's snooping. I had only spoken to her one time and I knew less than nothing when I did.

Over to South Fifth Plaza and the adjacent house to what had been a crime scene only a handful of days ago. Rat-a-tat-tat on the Blake front door and soon Gladys appeared in a housecoat. The sounds of her two kids floated in the background.

"Well, aren't you a sight for sore eyes? I never thought I'd see you again."

"Hi, Gladys. I'm back to ask you a few more questions if that's all right?"

"You never finished questioning me the last time, if I recall. Do come in."

"Is your husband at home?"

"Patrick is still at work and won't be back for hours."

She licked her lips and sashayed inside. On this occasion, I reminded myself to stick to the business at hand, no matter what Gladys may think. She placed her foot on the first step of the stairs as I headed toward the living room.

"Oh, what a shame."

"I wanted to check on a few details about Kole Langchamp."

"Maybe later then."

No answer was the best response and I opened the door at the same moment that two little 'uns sprinted past, through the kitchen, and out into the backyard. Silence descended on the house.

"They saved me locking them in their rooms."

With the way Gladys behaved, I couldn't tell if she was joking or serious.

"On Sunday night, you told me you spotted a woman walking around the Langchamp house. Is that right?"

"Yes, that's true. Do you fancy some coffee?"

Her housecoat opened a few inches. She'd played this ruse before with me, but she wasn't in the right ballpark this time. I kept my head in the game.

"No, thanks. Can you recall what the woman looked like?"

"I told you before it was too dark."

"Her hair? Was it blond, black, brown…?"

"It wasn't a light color, but I don't know what shade. It was nighttime, Jake."

"How tall did she seem?"

"Average, I suppose, but she wasn't standing straight. She was hunched up, trying to make herself as small as possible so she wouldn't be seen."

"But you spotted her, didn't you? That takes eagle eyes."

"You think?"

"Oh, yes. Was she wearing anything?"

"She wasn't naked, Jake. What kind of people do you think we are?"

I smiled.

"That's not what I meant. Was the woman wearing anything out of the ordinary? Did she have a brightly colored coat, for example?"

"There wasn't a coat. I remember being surprised by that because it was at night and the temperature had dropped on Sunday."

Gladys's internal thermometer was accurate; Sunday night was four degrees cooler than Saturday.

"Jacket?"

"I guess so, but I can't be sure."

"Skirt or slacks?"

"Skirt. She wasn't one of those tomboys."

"Did it match the jacket?"

"Of course not. She wasn't rustling around the Langchamp place in a suit."

Gladys laughed again, and her housecoat opened another three inches. She definitely had something on offer, but I didn't possess the inclination on this occasion.

"Is a coffee still on offer?"

"For sure. I'll be right back."

As she stood up, she tightened her coat before going to make the drinks. While she was out in the kitchen, I took a second opportunity to peer out of the window to remind myself of how much Gladys could have seen on Sunday night. I also wandered around the room until I found an ashtray.

When she came back with a tray, my cigarette was already halfway finished. I watched her eyes stare at it, but she made no comment.

"Milk? Sugar?"

"Straight up, thank you."

"I remember now. You just like it hot and wet."

She placed a plate of cookies near my elbow and sat back down. I considered taking one but realized it would only be out of politeness as Sylvia had done such an excellent job with my lunch.

"Is there anything else about the woman you can think of that you might not have mentioned last time?"

"Because we were busy with other matters?"

"Exactly right. As we had different things on our minds."

She stared into space for five long seconds.

"Nothing springs to mind, Jake."

"And tell me again about the visitors you saw who came to the house in the preceding weeks."

"They were almost always men, which is not normal for a husband and wife."

"What do you mean?"

"Well, couples socialize with couples. It's the way of the world."

I stopped to consider Gladys's point.

"Are you telling me the men were in pairs too?"

"I have no idea what they all got up to in there. I don't own binoculars or anything like that. But the men did not look like they were gay."

"What do you mean?"

"If two men showed up together, they never stood like they were acquainted in that manner at all."

"More business partners than anything else."

"That's what I'm trying to tell you."

She sighed with relief that I'd finally understood and wasn't proposing what she thought was something unsavory. Me? I'd visited San Francisco and grew up in New York, so I had more relaxed views on the matter.

To be honest, what Gladys had ignored was that if everyone was normal, then three men and one woman could have had one hell of a good time, but I didn't want to sully her memories of Kole Langchamp with such salacious suggestions.

"Did the same men appear every time?"

"Some were new, and some were repeats."

"And were these the people who turned up for those weekend house parties?"

"No, that was a different crowd. They were couples."

"And you said they were mainly men. When women appeared, did they come with a man? What was their story?"

Gladys stopped to think again. I had reframed the conversation, and she needed time for her memory to catch up.

"There was only one, now I think about it some more."

"Just one woman during the week. Did she come with anyone, or was she alone?"

"She wasn't with anybody. I remember thinking that was unusual; couples socialize with couples."

"Any description for me?"

"Average height, hair all over the place. There were too many colors in her clothes. Gaudy. Bright, but not in a good way."

It sounded like Franny Kennard.

"Were both members of the Langchamp household there to receive her?"

"Avril opened the door to her, but I can't remember seeing Kole there too. If he was inside, I couldn't say. It was too long ago, and I never kept that close an eye on them."

I smiled on the inside. For a woman who wasn't bothered about what happened with her neighbors, Gladys had a tremendous recall of inconsequential events several weeks later.

"So when you said earlier that couples socialize with couples, how sure are you Kole was in all those other times when men came to the door and Avril let them in?"

She sipped her coffee and tilted her head in thought.

"Now you ask me, I have no idea. Avril may have received male visitors when she was alone in the evening."

"That is very interesting," I mused.

Gladys puffed her chest out again in excitement, and the coat parted in the middle.

"I'm glad I can help. The police only spent a minute at the door with me before moving on to the next house. You're the only person who has taken me seriously."

"The officers who do the house-to-house canvassing have numerous people to speak to and a limited amount of time."

"They're more interested in getting to the next donut, you mean?"

"You might well be right."

"I'm guessing you have friends in the police, Jake."

"One or two. Most of the time, private investigators and police detectives don't get along."

"A man like you must show them up all the time."

"Not quite, but I have my moments."

I stood up to leave because Gladys's focus had shifted away from recalling guests at the Langchamp residence and moved to a different place altogether. A glance at the parting housecoat told me I should head for the door, otherwise, I'd be fleeing the building half-dressed for a second time. Once was bad luck, more than one time is just terrible planning on my part.

"Do come back if you have any more questions, Jake."

My hand was on the front door handle.

"That I shall, Gladys."

She stroked my arm with a finger and flicked an earlobe.

"Come back if you have no questions at all and only want some company."

"Send my regards to Patrick."

She folded her arms and exhaled in disgust as I escaped out of her lair.

33

AS I WAS prepared to go haul over the old coals of Gladys Blake, I figured it was worth my time to hop back to Malibu and discover what else there was to know about Julius Warner. Part of me wondered where he was and another possibility I wanted to investigate was whether he might be the missing murderer of the Kennards. Just because Lou said the cops believed the siblings had died by a woman's hand didn't mean they were right.

Now that I knew I'd be visiting a trailer park, I was less concerned about looking Malibu-casual and went directly from Gladys's door to the place itself. I only stopped at a diner along the way for a cup of java to keep me going.

I parked within inches of the spot I used last time I called on Warner. This visit, I stomped straight to his trailer, but again, there was nobody home. I peeked inside and saw that not a single item had been touched since I had pulled the place apart. Wasting no more time, I pootled around to the nearest trailers to see if I'd have any luck with Julius's neighbors.

A pink trailer stood about one hundred feet down a path and I used my knuckles to make a rat-a-tat on the door. A bustle inside and a guy in a T-shirt and jeans appeared in a window.

"What are you making that racket for?"

"I'm sorry to bother you, but I'm looking for Julius Warner. Do you know him?"

"Of course I do."

The man vanished from sight and the door opened five seconds later.

"What do you want with him?"

"Just trying to find the guy."

"Are you a cop?"

His old face scrunched up.

"No, I am not a police officer."

He relaxed.

"We don't take kindly to cops around these parts."

"In Malibu?"

"No, fella. You are a dumb one. I'm talking about in this park."

I glanced left and right to encourage his paranoia.

"Any idea where Julius is right now?"

"Have you tried his trailer?"

"That was the first place I looked."

"If he ain't there, then I've got no clue where he is, mister."

"Shame. I'm employed by an insurance company. One of Mr. Warner's relatives has died and left him a tidy sum. If I can get hold of him and we sort out the paperwork, then he'll be in clover."

"That's a lovely story, but no matter how pretty your tale, I don't know Julius's whereabouts."

"Would you be kind enough to give me a description of the gentleman? My office has given me scant information to go on."

"He's a small guy; four or five inches shorter than you. There were times I reckoned he didn't look after himself. There was so little to him."

I tipped my hat at the old curmudgeon and figured I'd try another trailer on the other side of the path. Another knock, another flicker of curtains. This time a woman appeared at the door. With a smile on my behalf, she stepped out to hold the conversation about Julius Warner.

"And did you know Julius well?"

"Not really. He was quite a private man; stayed in his trailer most of the time he was around here."

"Did he have anywhere else to live?"

"No, but we'd notice him for a few weeks and then he'd go off somewhere for a month. Drifting, I imagine."

"Has he been gone long? He isn't around, according to someone over there."

I pointed at the first trailer I'd stopped at and the woman laughed.

"You shouldn't listen to anything that Arthur says. He's out of his mind."

"He was lucid a moment ago."

"Come to think of it, I don't suppose I have seen Julius for a few days."

"Does that imply that you saw him last week then?"

"Yes, we spoke on Wednesday."

"Did he mention he was planning a trip?"

"Not at all, but he never tells you before he leaves. I'm not sure he has any idea himself until he wakes up in the morning, packs a bag, and off he goes."

"And what about his wife?"

"Huh?"

"Have you ever met her?"

"On a couple of occasions over the last year."

My ears pricked up.

"What's she like?"

"She had a thick accent."

"Like she came from the Bronx?"

"No, not like that. She sounded as though she was born somewhere in Europe."

"And you girls spent time together?"

"Oh no, she hardly said anything, but she was never alone with me and when she spoke, she was hard to understand. I think she was quiet because she was embarrassed about the way she sounded."

THE LURE OF Betsy's coffee and cake drew me to the diner, and I wanted to sit down and have a think anyway. When I walked in, I couldn't find her anywhere and I slunk over to a table by the window. Then she appeared from the restrooms and I smiled, but she looked right through me.

Even in a backwater like this, she must meet hundreds of customers a week, so I didn't feel too bad. The next thing I knew, a presence loomed toward me and there was her smile and name badge.

"Hello there, stranger."

"Hi, Betsy. How are you doing?"

"All's good here, thanks. What can I get you?"

I placed my order, and she hustled away, returning with a steaming hot mug in seconds, but the cake took a little longer to rustle up.

"Is there anything else you need, Jake?"

"You remembered my name."

"Only for my special customers."

She winked, and I knew she was lying. Betsy recalled the size of my tip and nothing more.

"Sometimes you say the nicest things. Tell me, do you recall a guy breezing through here called Julius Warner?"

"It's unusual, but I don't reckon I've come across anyone of that name."

"A slight man, a few inches shorter than me."

I gave her as complete a picture as I had of Warner's features.

"Oh, you mean Chuck."

"Do I?"

"Yes, he's one of our regulars. Comes in weekend mornings and at least once or twice in the week too."

"Always for breakfast?"

"Pretty much, yes."

"Has he been in this week?"

Betsy shifted her weight from one foot to the other and leaned on the table with a knuckle.

"No, now that you mention it."

"Any idea when was the last time you bumped into him?"

"It must have been Thursday, I reckon."

"You're sure?"

"Not to stake my life on it, but certain enough."

I planted a forkful of cheesecake into my mouth and tried to be as casual as I could with my next question.

"Did he ever come in with his wife?"

"What? No. I mean, he wasn't married."

"How do you know?"

"Women can tell these things, Jake."

"Female intuition?"

"That and single men look at a girl differently. Chuck wasn't like that. Besides, there was no wedding ring."

"Ever consider the possibility that he was a better man than average and just didn't wear a ring?"

"Jake, all men are average when you wear a uniform with a knee-length skirt."

She had a point.

"And he wore rings, just not a wedding band."

"You notice those kinds of things?"

"He had an enormous gold ring with a rectangle split in two. One half had a pattern, and the other had a diamond sunk right in the middle. Chuck, I mean Julius, liked jewelry."

Betsy had an expert eye for detail. If she ever wanted to stop waitressing, I'd have hired her in an instant as a surveillance operative.

"Can you recollect anything he said the last time you saw him?"

"Nothing springs to mind. What sort of thing are you interested in?"

"Did he mention that he was planning on taking a trip somewhere? A vacation maybe."

"No, but it's not like I asked him either. Thursday was a busy morning. A convoy of truckers stopped by and we were rushed off our feet. That's how I know it was Thursday when he came in because I had no time to chat."

"Is he a talkative soul?"

"Julius doesn't spill his guts about everything that's on his mind, if that's what you mean. But he's a nice guy to have a conversation with while he orders eggs, bacon, and a slice of toast."

"Is that his usual?"

She nodded and glanced around the room.

"Sorry, Jake, but I've got other tables to take care of."

A glance at my watch told me I'd need to head back if I were to have a chance of catching Sylvia before she left for the evening. I tried to reach her on the diner's phone, but I was too late. That much-fabled drink was going to be delayed for another twenty-four hours.

FRIDAY

34

WHAT I WANTED was to visit Ed, but that wasn't an option as I would have needed to fly to Chicago and there was no need for me to put in that much effort. All I wanted was to speak with my dead friend.

So I went for the next best thing: a trip to a synagogue I knew on 55th and Hoover. The way I saw it, if Ed was going to be anywhere, he would probably be easiest to get to in a temple. The man wasn't a frequent attendee when he was alive, but being dead, he might have changed his mind. None of this made any sense.

When I arrived in the main hall, some guy handed over a skullcap, which I put on. I recalled wearing one for Ed's funeral to keep Veronica's family happy. Here I was sitting on a bench in a place of worship that meant nothing to me, so I could talk the case through with Ed Schwartz.

My head dropped. The trouble with visiting religious buildings is that I never knew what to do with my hands. This synagogue was no exception. I plopped them on my knees, but they felt conspicuously useless. Next, I shoved them in my pants pockets, but that was uncomfortable. Then it dawned on me that I should clasp them together in front of me as though I was engulfed in deep prayer. That was as good as it was going to get.

There were at least two men in the periphery of my vision, so I closed my eyes to blot them out of my consciousness.

Ed, the problem with this case is that the suspect list is getting smaller by the day. I had one person who I reckoned had killed AJ's husband out of jealousy. Great motive and she was unhinged under normal circumstances. But she's popped off this mortal coil too. Perhaps you've met her, as you are both dead. Franny Kennard?

I waited for some sign from Ed that he was best of friends with my number one suspect, but nothing occurred.

Then there's the matter of her brother, Elmo. Before he was murdered, he had some kind of relationship with AJ, but I'm not sure if it was just business or if AJ had something going on the side with him behind Kole's back.

I sighed and wondered if this was helping me any.

And the most confusing thing is that my client might have had two husbands. Kole and Julius. One is dead, and the other is in the wind. I haven't had time to check on Kole's paperwork, but I've seen Julius's certificate, although that may be fake. If AJ was running a scam with Elmo, then she might be capable of creating false documents. Perhaps she was operating a different fraud with Julius.

I heard a creaking sound and assumed that Ed was trying to communicate with me from beyond the grave. When I opened my eyes, a guy was sitting down on the other side of the room. Less divine intervention and more uncomfortable seating.

The one certainty I have is that AJ is at the center of this entire fiasco. There are three corpses, Ed, and two of them appeared after I was hired. That is not the batting average a detective should be hitting.

"You know what to do, Jake. When everyone is dying around you, the only person who could be found guilty of a crime has to be on the list of those who are still alive."

So that boils down to AJ and Julius as the only contenders, although one of them might not be responsible for all three deaths. Perhaps AJ did for Kole just as she confessed whereas Julius took care of Elmo. Franny killed herself, or Julius sorted her out to make it appear like a suicide.

Then I recalled the advice Ed had given me on more than one occasion. If it looks like a camel and smells like a camel, then it probably has a hump and spits.

I Confess

A rustling sound to my left and I opened my eyes to see what was going on. A gray-bearded man had sat down two spaces away from me. We glanced at each other but remained silent.

"We haven't seen you here before."

I felt no need to confirm what he already knew, especially as there was no point in the conversation in the first place.

"I ask because your hands were clasped in supplication, but your lips didn't move a muscle. This made me think you weren't praying at all."

"Maybe I came here for some peace and quiet."

"Perhaps, in which case I have destroyed your calm."

"That would be correct."

The man smiled and stroked his beard.

"Is there anything you'd like to know before I walk out of here?"

More stroking of the beard.

"While you are most welcome to remain here as long as you wish, you don't look as though you are a regular attendee at synagogues."

"You are correct. My friend was Jewish but I am not. I came here to be closer to him, as he is buried in Chicago."

"My thoughts are with you. Did he leave a family behind?"

"A wife only. No children."

"That is a shame."

"Not so much. Their relationship was heading to the rocks before he died."

"In our religion, we view those who are no longer with us as starting the next phase of their lives. We don't see death as the end."

"That shows I'm not of your faith."

He smiled, nodded, and left me alone after that to close my eyes again and ponder.

An image popped into my mind from the first moment AJ walked into my inner sanctum. Her wedding finger. Or rather, the ring itself. I only saw it for a second or two, but I remember thinking that it didn't fit very well. I needed to speak to a jeweler.

━━ ━━

THERE WAS A Harry Winston store on Fifth Street and South Broadway that had been there since before I first visited the City of Angels. I hopped inside and walked around the labyrinthine aisles until I spotted Fabian Snyder.

"Oh, it's you."

"Is that any way to greet a customer, Fabian?"

"Not at all, Jake. But we both know you aren't here to buy anything."

"Not a bracelet or necklace, although there may be something in it for you if you can help me."

"I'll bite, Jake. If only for old times' sake. What do you need?"

"A few moments of your time and for you to shed some light based on your vast experience."

"Spill, Jake. There'll be customers to serve any minute now."

We both looked around the joint and knew that wasn't true, but I was here to squeeze some information out of the guy and not to argue.

"Suppose you saw a woman wearing a ring that moved up and down her finger."

"When she played with it, you mean?"

"No, as she shifted her hand from, say, being by her side onto her lap."

"You don't need me to tell you it wasn't fitting properly."

"Fabian, if I told you it was a wedding band and that the woman had been married several years. Would you change your tune then?"

"Did you see how it could move about?"

"There was a weld on either side of the ring, only an extra quarter of an inch, but it created a gap nonetheless."

"Jake, how long did you say the woman was married?"

"I didn't give you a number. Why?"

"A groove on a finger takes years to form and if she wears a narrower wedding band now, then either she lost the first one…"

"…or it was from a different marriage."

"You're the detective, not me. All I know is gold. Do you think this woman wants to sell her ring?"

"I doubt it, but I will ask when I meet her again."

"Mighty kind, Jake."

"You know that I always have your interests at heart, Fabian."

"Is there anything else I can help you with or is the beady eye I'm getting from the floor manager only going to get more intense over the next five minutes?"

"I'm done, Fabian. You have been very helpful. Let me know when you are free and I'll pay for a slap-up meal somewhere fancy."

"You said that the last time you breezed in here and I am still waiting for the dinner date."

"I am nothing if not consistent, Fabian."

He swatted me away like I was a fly and I headed out the door.

35

I LEFT THE Harry Winston store and tried to leave the memories of Ed behind, but I didn't succeed. His face haunted me as I hopped into my car and headed back to my inner sanctum. With more questions than answers, I had nowhere else to go. Sylvia took one glance at me and poured a coffee before I sat down.

"You want your newspaper?"

"Not right now. Thanks to this case, my mind is all over the place."

She nodded, but her expression showed she had no idea what I was talking about. I wasn't surprised. With my feet perched on the corner of my desk, I folded my arms over my chest and closed my eyes.

A line-up of all the people I had met since starting the case appeared in my mind's eye. I noted the curl of their lips, the color of their pupils, everything. But there was one character who I couldn't place at all. His face was a blur, and I wasn't even sure how tall he was. Then he walked past and the rest of the personalities stepped back.

I opened my eyes wide and blinked at the brightness of my surroundings. The out-of-focus man was the key to this entire situation, and I needed to speak with him. I leaped out of my chair and headed downstairs to find Julius Warner.

THE TREES AROUND Warner's trailer were quiet; not a single leaf rustled in the light breeze. I scouted around the joint and found the neighbors were asleep or away because the entire area was as still as a grave. I circled back to Warner's trailer and peeked through a window, but there was still no sign of life.

The inside was exactly the same as I had left it. If Warner had returned to his nest, then he had done a mighty fine job of hiding that fact. Although I didn't know him at all, I doubted he was so wily as to tiptoe around his mess to conceal his occupation.

I had zoomed past Betsy's cheesecake to stand in a stinking trailer and find nothing. A blue funk descended on my shoulders and I slumped down onto the bench in the living area. As soon as my tuchus had hit the poorly padded seat, a voice rang out from outside.

"You in there?"

I reached for my gun before answering.

"Who's that?"

A moment's silence. "It's me wanting my rent."

I popped my head around the door to see a man in his fifties with a brown beard and blue jeans. He eyed me as suspiciously as I stared at him.

"You're not Julius."

"Neither are you."

He ground his molars and put his hand in his pocket. I tightened my grip on the butt of my revolver. Only my head was visible to the world.

"What are you doing in Julius's trailer?"

"I'm in the middle of an investigation, which involves Julius Warner."

"You a cop?"

I flashed my badge, and the guy relaxed enough for me to remove my hand from the pistol and step outside. As I did so, he craned his neck to get a look inside.

"How much does he owe you?"

"Three months' rent."

I whistled.

"How long before you evict him?"

"A matter of days, mister."

"Jake Adkins. And you are…?"

"Rick Parker. Pleased to make your acquaintance."

"Has Julius skipped out on you before?"

"He comes and goes. Usually, he tells me if he's off on one of his trips so that I can keep an eye on his place while he's gone."

"My understanding is that Julius left about a week ago."

"Sounds fair. I reckon he departed the day after I asked him for what's owed."

"You think the two events are connected?"

"Hard to say, Jake. It wasn't the first time that I had to remind him of his duties under his contract, but on previous occasions, I'd only been chasing one month of back pay."

"If you don't mind me asking, why did you give him so much leeway this time?"

"He fed me a sob story which I believed and he promised me he was about to come into some money."

"Did he mention where it was coming from?"

"He was vague, but it came across as a typical Julius tale about some relative dying and an inheritance on its way. To be honest, when people sing me a song about payments, I tend not to listen to the tune."

"It's the green in your palm that counts."

"Jake, you understand me completely."

"We all have to deal with difficult customers in our lives and there's nothing worse than being lied to."

"Were you in the war, son?"

I nodded.

"Then you know there's lots worse than an untruth, but I agree that a man is nothing if you don't got his word."

I felt for Julius. Down to his last dime, chased by his landlord, and married to a woman who had jumped the broom with some other fella. I'd have skipped town too. There was nothing else to say to Parker, so I mooched around the trailer park for a few minutes hoping I might find a neighbor I hadn't spoken to before, but no joy.

Instead, I went back to the main road and swung by for a slice of Betsy's cheesecake and a coffee.

36

BACK IN THE city, I wondered what I was missing, apart from finding Julius, of course. Then it struck me. I'd been so focused on Julius that I had forgotten an important detail about Elmo. And I was prepared to put money on the fact that the police had missed the same thing too.

I hightailed it over to the residential block and played doorbell ditch until someone let me in and I hopped back to the hallway outside Elmo's apartment. I turned around and rang Ursula Varley's door.

Silence. I checked my watch because as a detective, I operate on a different timeline from most people and forget that five in the morning or eleven at night is the wrong time to hold a conversation.

With my ear pressed against the door, I rang the bell again and thought I heard some rustling. She was in but in no hurry to respond to cold callers. I stepped back a pace so she could recognize me when she eventually peered through the peephole. A cigarette hung from the corner of my mouth while I waited.

It was another twenty seconds before the door swung open and those piercing eyes looked straight at me.

"It's you. What do you want?"

Reading between the lines, I could tell she was happy to see me but hid that emotion behind searing contempt and disgust.

"I'd like to ask you a couple of follow-up questions, if you don't mind?"

A glance to the other side of her apartment and a shrug.

"Come in then. But say what you must and leave. I have no time for anything else."

I nodded and followed her to the living room, where she gestured at a chair for me to sit down. Another glance and I wondered whether we were alone. It would explain why she didn't fancy me hanging around for too long.

"So, what do you want to know?"

"Would it be possible to get a coffee?"

She shook her head.

"I told you I have little time for you today. Let's get on with it."

I glanced around the living room for an ashtray and couldn't spot one. She tutted, hustled to the kitchen, and returned with a crystal monstrosity that her boss must have given her. There is no way anyone her age would have considered that thing to be an object of beauty. It was old-fashioned from the minute it was first created, and that was a while ago.

"Ursula, did the police interview you after they found Elmo was dead?"

"Yes."

"I mean, apart from their door-to-door questioning, did they come back and ask you for any more details beyond did you know Elmo and when did you last see him?"

She shuffled on her couch.

"No. Did you expect them to return?"

"The cops have their own way of working. It's not for me to suggest they didn't do their jobs properly."

Ursula glanced at the bedroom door. It was closed tight.

"And do you remember seeing or hearing anything from his apartment on the day Elmo died?"

She gazed at me and shook her head, palms resting on her lap.

"Did the police ask you for an alibi?"

"What do you mean, Jake?"

"Were you asked where you were when Elmo was killed?"

Her cheeks flushed, and she stared at her hands.

"Why would they want to know that?"

"It's standard procedure to find the whereabouts of everyone who knew the deceased."

"Well, they didn't ask me anything like that."

"That's good news for you. If there was even a hint of suspicion, they'd have come back."

"And yet, here you are."

"I'm not a cop. Just a guy trying to get by."

"You may be many things, Jake. But you're a private detective, so I don't believe you swung by for no reason. Do you believe I killed Elmo?"

A glistening bead of liquid seeped out of the corner of her eye. Before I could ask myself whether she'd switched on the faucet for my benefit, she whispered, "I loved him."

I stubbed out the remains of my cigarette and sat back in my chair. There's nothing better than people who give you answers to questions you never asked them.

"When we spoke last time, you didn't respond well to the suggestion that Elmo was seeing other women."

"No, not that. You were being impertinent, and that's what got my back up."

"Tell me, was he playing under the sheets with other women that you knew about?"

"Why yes. We both understood the situation we were in."

Another glance to the bedroom.

"He deserved his diversions when I wasn't around and the same for me too."

If Ursula checked on that bedroom door one more time, I swore to myself that I would walk over and open it to save her from staring any further.

"You mean when you were having fun with your boss?"

"That sort of thing, yes. Elmo knew I spent part of my life with Charlie and I told him he either had to accept it or leave."

"Which did he go for?"

"You can be a real heel sometimes, Jake. We were happy when we were together."

A squint at the bedroom. Had the door just opened slightly?

"And the rest of your time was spent with Charlie?"

She nodded and scooted over to kneel by my chair.

"Charlie takes care of me." Then much softer. "But Elmo cared about me. Do you understand the difference?"

Now it was my turn to check the door, but it hadn't moved an inch. If Charlie was eavesdropping, then he'd heard nothing to get Ursula into trouble. The conversation continued in a whisper.

"Did Charlie know about you and Elmo?"

"Oh no. That would never do. He'd have got angry. He likes to believe that he has sole possession of me."

"Does he ever lash out?"

"Charlie? He shouts and bellows, but that's as far as it goes."

"Sounds like a great guy to work for."

"He lets his emotions get the better of him, but he is all talk and not much else."

"There must be more to him for you to want to keep the man in your bed."

We both glanced at the bedroom door.

"Look around this joint. The only thing I could afford on my salary is the cereal in the kitchen cupboard. I take care of some of his needs and he ensures I live in the manner to which I've become accustomed."

One word you could always use about Ursula was that she was consistent. She'd plucked at that tune the last time I was around.

"Is there anything else you want?"

With her lips only inches away from mine, I must admit I allowed myself a flight of fancy but came clattering down to earth a moment later. In my mind, I had replaced Elmo in her life, but that would never happen. I imagined Charlie, lying self-satisfied in Ursula's bed, and decided it was time to head for the door.

"If you think of anything, let me know."

I handed her one of my cards and headed back to the office.

37

I GOT TO my inner sanctum in record time, but there was no one to be seen. As I sat at my desk, a note fluttered to the floor that had been placed on the edge of the wood veneer.

Gone home early as nothing for me to do. S.

Sylvia knew I didn't care about her working hours as long as the clients were happy and there were coffee grounds ready for the pot. But today was not the day to take advantage of my flexible work practices. I called her home number, but there was no reply. The chances were that she was stuck in traffic somewhere between here and there.

I threw my jacket back on and zipped down to my car. Then out of the parking lot and I headed over to Sylvia's apartment.

I PARKED OUTSIDE the building and hustled to the main entrance. A quick buzz on the button next to Sylvia's name and she let me in. It must have been the first time in days since I arrived at a residential block and didn't have to finagle my way inside.

A rat-a-tat-tat on her door and a few seconds later, Sylvia appeared in a housecoat.

"Come in, Jake. I hope you don't mind, but I could have hung around the office waiting for you to return, which might not have happened until tomorrow, or…"

Inside, I smiled because a single girl shouldn't let her boss into her home without getting dressed first. I reckon I understood how Charlie felt.

"No explanations required, Sylvia. You did the right thing, but just not on the right day. I need your help."

"I'm here for you, Jake."

She pouted her lips for a second and wandered into her living room. Was I reading something in her behavior that wasn't there, or was she giving off signals to me? I couldn't tell and my mind was occupied with other matters.

"I went back to interview Ursula Varley because I thought she might have killed Elmo Kennard. It turns out that she loved the dope. Her boss had a bigger reason to take out the fella, but I doubt if he has the cajónes. He's a white-collar guy, who throws his weight around with young women, but his type tend not to be men of action."

Sylvia patted the back of her couch and I sat down. I'd blurted all this out while still standing.

"Coffee?"

I shook my head as I wanted to keep my train of thought and Sylvia sat beside me.

"Where does that leave the case, Jake?"

"That's the thing. I've been skirting around this mess for too long now without addressing the central truth."

"What's that?"

"AJ killed Kole. She told me that within the first minute we met and I got it into my head that this was some kind of ruse on her part. For a reason I can't explain, I couldn't believe that a woman as beautiful as her could have carried out such a heinous act."

"But she did?"

"Yes. Of course, she was the killer. We always knew that, but I'd tried to find someone else to pin the wrap on instead of her."

"Did she do for the others?"

"That is harder for me to say. Franny Kennard seemed good for Kole and there's not much evidence either way for Elmo. That leaves Julius Warner."

"Did you speak with him?"

"No. The bottom line is that nobody has seen him since last week. It is almost as if he vanished around the same time as Kole was murdered."

"And he was married to AJ, right?"

"According to the piece of paper I found in Julius's trailer but there's no way of knowing whether it is a fake certificate. AJ was committing fraud, so who can tell what bits of paperwork are real or not."

"What would you like me to do, Jake?"

As Sylvia said this, her housecoat opened an inch or two and I thought I saw the shadowy outline of a pair of silk pajamas. She wiped her tongue around her lips and tilted her head to one side, waiting for my answer.

"I need to know more."

"About what?"

"Why would a woman do a bad thing?"

"If she wanted it enough or if the prize was worth it."

She lit a cigarette and puffed slowly. My eyes trailed down to the gap between the sides of her housecoat and the promise of the pink nightclothes.

"You've never been married, have you, Sylvia?"

"No, not yet."

"Have you ever been in a relationship that you wanted to get out of?"

"You know that already. I'm a gal who just split up from her fella and you still owe me that drink. Fancy a Scotch?"

"Not right now, thanks. But don't let that stop you if you want one. We are sitting in your home, after all."

Sylvia's eyes darted over to the sideboard, but she did not get up.

"How far would you go to extricate yourself from a wicked man?"

She laughed.

"Is your question whether I'd murder my boyfriend rather than give him a Dear John letter?"

"I guess so. Imagine if you were married."

"Does that make a difference, Jake?"

"Hard for me to say. I've never jumped the broom with anyone."

"Yet here you are hitting me with the same questions."

I shrugged. I wasn't too sure if I was asking her to put herself in AJ's shoes or if I wanted to find out how she'd dump me if we ever got it together. Those silk pajamas were hard to ignore. If I didn't know better, I would have sworn that she just puffed her chest out at me.

"Are you sure you don't fancy that drink, Jake?"

"We need to find out if Kole and AJ were married for real."

"What?"

A glance at my watch showed me how early Sylvia had skipped work.

"I want you to go to the records office and check the marriage certificate for AJ and Kole, assuming it exists."

"Huh?"

"Put some clothes on and get over there now. I'm going to do the same with Julius and AJ. We can meet up in a couple of hours in the inner sanctum."

You don't need to be a genius to know that if I'd accepted that Scotch from Sylvia, then we'd have got intimate in her bedroom before the night was out. Thinking about Ursula and Charlie made me realize it was more important to get to the truth about AJ than to get under the covers with Sylvia and harm that relationship.

She sure looked pretty in pink, though.

38

IF YOU NEED to find out where to go in a town, you ask a cop, but if you want the full skinny on a place, then grab a copy of the newspaper. For me, the best source was Elliot Magee, a senior reporter at The LA Globe.

To find out the hidden details of AJ's life, there was nowhere better to go than his offices. I phoned first because the guy could be anywhere in the state if he was chasing a story, but I was lucky and he invited me over for a chat.

"How are you doing, Jake?"

"Just fine, Elliot. I'm working a case and came across an angle you might be interested in."

"Oh?"

He glanced at me over his horn-rimmed glasses as he quaffed his coffee.

"Yeah, see, I've uncovered a real estate fraud that involves some of Jack Dragna's properties."

He sat up on hearing that name. Everyone in the city did; we couldn't help ourselves.

"What's the scoop?"

"There's a man and a woman who've been selling Dragna's residences multiple times to different parties."

"Under his nose?"

"Looks like it, Elliot. Have you heard any whisper about this?"

He beamed at me. The guy was the best crime reporter in the city, according to his own reviews, anyway.

"You think I don't know about it?"

"I check out your byline every day and you haven't run with anything on this that I've seen. So, are you on the case or not, Elliot?"

"Jake, you got me. None of my sources have mentioned this to me. When can I get the details?"

"If you help me out today, then you'll be able to publish the piece on Monday, but I've got my own business to take care of first. Understood?"

"Embargoed until one minute past midnight."

"Good news, and thank you. Like I said, there's a couple, but I can't be sure if they are married. I have no interest in the fraud, although the cops will when I present them with the evidence..."

"...after I publish."

"Exactly. All I want to know is whether the marriage certificate is worth the paper it's written on."

"Why do you care about the pair?"

"One of them is my client whose husband was murdered."

"So you know she was married?"

"Elliot, you assume the guy who's dead is the potential spouse involved in the fraud and I never said that."

"What a tangled web, Jake."

"Tell me about it, my friend."

"So run through what the hell is going on."

■■ ■■

WITHIN TEN MINUTES, I had given Elliot the sum total of what I knew. Or rather, of the information I wanted him to know. The guy was a reporter and had ways of finagling dope about people out of thin air. Give him a gun and he'd have the makings of an excellent detective.

"What's the dame's name? You've been careful not to reveal your hand, Jake."

"If I give her up, do you promise not to start typing until next week?"

"You've already had my word."

"Avril Langchamp. Mean anything to you?"

"Can't say that it does. She's the one who's been making money out of Dragna?"

"Looks like it."

"Have you got any evidence?"

"No confessions or a signed affidavit, but I do have documents you can put together to add up to real estate fraud."

"When will you hand them over to me?"

"Over the weekend, once my business is complete."

"Why not today?"

"If I don't get everything tied up in a pretty bow before the end of today, then a killer will walk free."

"Murder beats fraud."

"Every day of the week."

"Remind me again, Jake, why you are gifting me this story?"

"I need you to do some digging on Avril Langchamp. You scratch my back and I'll scratch yours. You know the score."

"Sure do. What details do you have?"

"Two potential husbands in the form of Kole Kennard and Julius Warner. At least one is dead and unless I miss my guess, they are both deceased. Can you use the Globe library to confirm whether AJ was married to either of them for real or were these happy families nothing more than a tale to tell for the scam?"

"How long are you giving me?"

I glanced at my watch and decided I'd test his reaction.

"If I come back in an hour, will you be done?"

"Jake Adkins. You're asking a lot of a poorly paid newspaperman."

"I've rummaged through your trash enough times to know the Globe takes care of you well, so don't give me that sob story. Besides, the longer we talk, then the less time you get to find out how many husbands AJ had."

I HOPPED OUT to a nearby diner and whiled away the wait with a coffee and a roast beef sandwich. There was just enough time for a slice of cake before I had to return to Elliot's office.

As I walked toward him, his expression made me think he'd been to a funeral. I flopped into the chair next to his and turned to face him.

"Looks like you know a thing or two more about Avril Langchamp."

"Uh-huh."

"Are you going to let me in on your secret?"

"Reckon I might as well. You've got yourself a bigamist."

"And not a Mormon in sight."

"No jokes, Jake. We ran both weddings in our society pages."

"Who was first up the aisle?"

"Warner, then Kennard six months later."

"How come nobody spotted that the Warners were already hitched?"

"It's not like anyone sends out a private eye to do a background check. You make a few statements, tick a bunch of boxes and wait for someone to ask if anybody knows of a reason the couple gathered here shouldn't jump the broom. Silence for a second, and then move on with the rest of the ceremony."

I swallowed hard. Did AJ separate from Warner to get away from the heat that was building up around their Dragna fraud and use Kole to leave her old identity behind her?

"I don't know if it is relevant, but she married Warner in Malibu and Kennard in Los Angeles County."

"Two districts, so there wouldn't even be a chance that a records clerk would remember her from half a year before."

"One smart chickadee."

"Have there been any sightings of Warner this week? He's vanished off the face of the earth."

"Not that I saw, but I wasn't searching in our missing persons' files. That would have taken way longer than the hour you gave me."

"Elliot, I don't care if he's missing, only if he has been found."

"That's the opposite of what our lost souls' department is all about. It's the place we go to when we've given up finding a contact alive or in LA."

"Are you telling me that Warner might have skipped the state, and we'd never know?"

"We would never be sure unless he was seen somewhere else and was reported to the police or a newswire."

"Do you have any pictures of the happy couples on their wedding days?"

Elliot rifled through a pile of papers on his desk. I had no idea how he kept anything straight in that debris in front of him. After a minute, he grabbed two photos and passed them over. AJ was beautiful in both shots.

"She's wearing the same dress."

"Why waste green? It's never the same the second time, so I'm told."

"How many times have you been married?"

"None, but a fella can talk to husbands and wives, can't he? It's not like you've got a string of divorces to your name."

"I've come close on more than one occasion, Elliot."

"Jake, with the greatest respect, sleeping with someone else's wife doesn't count."

My cheeks heated up, and I knew Elliot was right. I changed the subject.

"So, did you find out anything else about AJ?"

"No, and that is the strangest thing."

"What do you mean?"

"Before her marriage to Julius Warner, there's almost nothing official to show that she ever existed."

"She's a ghost?"

"That's not what I'm saying, although she might as well be. A month or so before the wedding, Avril Langchamp arrives in Malibu with Julius Warner, but there is no paperwork to suggest she'd spent a second longer in the country."

"She told me she came from France."

"There are no customs documents in any port I've found. AJ appeared out of nowhere and got married to Julius. If she was born in Europe, then she emigrated here a long time ago."

39

I PACED UP and down the inner sanctum, waiting for Sylvia to return. My head was buzzing with what Elliot had told me and all the implications this had for AJ. To keep myself from going crazy, I fussed around the coffee machine to make a brew. As I poured a mugful, Sylvia breezed into the room.

"Want a cup? I've just prepared a pot."

"No, thanks."

She dropped into the chair usually reserved for clients and waited for me to sit down, but I was too impatient.

"What did you find out?"

"While you were finding out about Julius, I went to work on Kole."

"And?"

Sylvia winked at me but refused to utter a word. Instead, she took a cigarette from the box on my desk and searched around for a light. I matched her and sat in my seat. The girl sure was milking her big scene.

"I unearthed the lawyer who is handling Kole Kennard's estate."

"What did he have to say for himself?"

"He refused to speak to me."

"What the…"

She held up a hand to stop me in my tracks.

"Sometimes, the word of an attorney is not enough."

"You reckon?"

"I told his secretary that I wanted to hire him to handle my brother's estate and he was keen to see me. Whenever I tried to bring up Kennard, he reminded me he couldn't talk about other clients, waffling on about confidentiality."

"Amazing that you bumped into the only honest lawyer this side of hell."

"Tell me about it. There were files and papers everywhere. All over his desk, the shelves. Even on the floor."

"So, we've an honest, but messy counsel. You still look like the cat that got the canary."

"I pretended to have a coughing fit and asked him to get me a glass of water with a slice of lemon."

"And he just followed your request?"

"Let's say there are things that men will do for women that they wouldn't dream of doing for another man."

"And the slice of lemon? You don't even like them."

"I know that, but he didn't. Besides, I needed something so my drink would take time to get sorted and if all I'd asked for was water, his secretary would have found that lickety-split."

"So you got the guy out of the room? Then what?"

"I rifled through every file and piece of paper I could lay my hands on. The piles might have appeared disorganized, but there was a system and I found the Kennard file in less than a minute."

"And what was in it?"

"You're the detective; you tell me."

I ground my molars and wondered what Sylvia was playing at. She grinned and yanked a bunch of folded papers out of her handbag, placing them on my desk and flattening them as she did so.

As soon as she put them down, I grabbed them and started reading.

"Won't he miss this?"

"I left the folder and took the contents. He's only going to find it when he pushes the paperwork some more. By that time, these will be in an evidence locker at the precinct, or we can post them back to him if we don't need them."

"No harm, no foul."

"Yep."

"Clever girl."

A quick scan of the sheets told me all I needed to know.

"There is only one beneficiary, and that's a sister in Wisconsin."

"Not AJ?"

"She isn't mentioned anywhere that I can see."

"That is peculiar."

"Strange if they were married."

"AJ and Kole were living in sin?"

"Residing in the same house. They occupied separate bedrooms when I checked the place out. We only have AJ's word that they were husband and wife."

"Did Elliot have anything about the marriages?"

"He told me that the Globe had reported on both ceremonies, but that doesn't mean there was a legal marriage at the end of the day."

"That sounds like a very complicated fraud AJ and Kole were operating."

"Or an elaborate ruse to reinforce their cover story and hold a party."

"What else did you get out of the Globe's ace crime reporter?"

"From what I can tell, Avril Langchamp appeared out of nowhere shortly before she arrived in Malibu and married Julius Warner."

Sylvia scrunched up her face.

"Huh?"

"You heard me right. There are no records of AJ's existence more than a handful of weeks before the marriage."

"That can't be."

"Probably not. It begs the question, who the hell she is. I mean, there is a French lilt to her voice, so I believe that part of her story."

"Could she be faking it?"

"Yes, but she's an excellent actress if she is. Her accent has been consistent all the times I've spoken with her."

"Her clothes were French too."

"Were they?"

"A girl knows about such things."

"Sylvia, it might not count as evidence, but I believe that much of what she's told us."

"Even though we know she is wrapped up in a real estate fraud?"

"If you're a professional liar, the trick is to keep as close to the truth as possible. Forgetting the details of your character trips people up, so using your own life makes it easier to stick to your story."

"And did you find out anything else from Elliot?"

"I can't be certain, but I'll bet that Julius Warner is no more."

"I thought you said he skipped town?"

"Yes, but he missed his Monday breakfast at his local diner and nobody has seen him since the weekend."

"The bodies keep piling up on this one."

"And AJ appears to be the last woman standing."

"She's killed them all?"

"Not sure. It could be her or perhaps the assailant is trying to pin the whole sorry mess on AJ. If we step back for a second, who has been the victim of AJ's actions?"

Sylvia shrugged.

"Franny?"

"No, it's Jack Dragna."

"And he has the resources to kill off anyone he wants in this town."

"You bet your ass he can. And does."

"Why not murder AJ too?"

"First, he's a vindictive sonofabitch, and second, who's saying he doesn't intend to whack her once she's spent some time in the cells?"

"That's cold."

"You don't get to be a mob boss by glad-handing and being photographed near babies."

Sylvia took a sip of her coffee and I gave her a minute to digest what I had said. All these deaths reeked of professional hits and Dragna was the one with the workforce to carry these out.

"Why would she confess to murdering Kole if it was Dragna all along?"

"Maybe she did in Kole and Dragna seized the opportunity for his revenge. Perhaps he leaned on her to take the hit for that murder, which was why she needed me when the DA rejected her case."

"That still doesn't explain where she came from."

"But it goes a long way to give a reason for her behavior."

"What are you going to do, Jake? She's paid us to prove her guilty."

"We have just enough evidence of the real estate fraud, two marriage certificates, at least one of which is fake, and a string of dead bodies. Lou will have no trouble convincing the district attorney that AJ did for Kole."

"That's not what she asked you to do."

"Sure, she wanted to be released on a technicality and I'll do my best to keep her involvement in the fraud under wraps. At least, until Monday's Globe hits the streets."

"You've leaked the story?"

"Let's just say I needed to offer a fair exchange to Elliot if I was going to get to the bottom of Julius Warner's situation."

Sylvia stared at me with those puppy-dog eyes.

"AJ has brought all this on herself. If she hadn't gotten tangled with Jack Dragna, then she wouldn't have been driven to murder in the first place. I'm doing what the client has paid me to do."

"It's the letter of the agreement, but not the spirit, Jake."

"That's as may be. I'm no lawyer, but I know that I've got to stay straight with Lou, otherwise, he'll have my license. And there's no getting away from that."

"Why not give her a chance to make good on all this?"

"Get her to confess, you mean?"

"Yes. If you convince her to go to the cops herself, then you'll have kept your license and not dropped your client in a world of hell."

Sylvia had a point, so I put on my jacket and headed out of the door.

40

I WHIPPED ROUND to AJ's home on South Fifth Plaza and found a house with no occupant. The sun was on the cusp of vanishing below the horizon as I scampered to the backyard and let myself in using a tool from Old Faithful. I decided to check out the one location I'd not been in before and used the internal door to enter the garage.

With a small torch clasped between my teeth, I rummaged around but only found pots of paint, oil, and the usual greasy dirt you'd expect in such a place. My hopes for an open safe with a folder containing a confession were dashed. It was worth a try.

Next, I turned my attention to the living room as there were several hidey-holes I could have missed. I opened each drawer in the sideboard and checked out every piece of paper and between the silverware, napkins, and other assorted items that live near a dining room table.

Nothing. I stood from my crouching position and stretched my back, wondering where to go now. There was no need to have bothered because in that instant a light went on. I swiveled round to see AJ standing next to a table lamp, a vast shadow of her head cast on the wall behind her.

"You let yourself in, I see, Mr. Adkins."

"It beat waiting for an invitation, as you weren't around. And call me Jake. Mr. Adkins was my father, and he died several years ago."

"I might not have any legal training, but I believe I have the right to shoot someone who has broken into my home."

"If you are in clear and present danger for your life."

"Feels pretty dangerous to me."

My shoulders sagged and my arms dangled by my side. The last thing I wanted to do was to make AJ the least bit twitchy, as she had a revolver trained on me throughout our conversation. A snub nose .32 if my eye didn't deceive me. The sort a woman could keep in her handbag until she needed to whip it out and plug someone.

"AJ, you are the one holding the piece. I am the person who is in danger."

"I have paid you to do a job, and you have failed."

"There's still a few more hours before Saturday and I believe I've found enough evidence to get the DA to prosecute you for the murder of Kole."

"Murder? I wanted a manslaughter charge."

"But that's not what happened, is it?"

"I didn't intend to kill him. Kole was being his usual annoying self, spouting his mouth off with big talk and no action. But it got to me on Sunday night and I lost control, just for a split second."

"So you killed the father of your child?"

"Don't be ridiculous. I lied to you about being pregnant to gain your sympathy."

There we were. I was standing by the sideboard as far from an exit as I could be. AJ had planted herself by the doorway leading in from the hallway and kept the gun pointing at my chest. We both heard a squeak and watched as the handle on the kitchen door turned. Joss Vipond entered the room holding his own piece. The back of my throat was so dry, I was about to retch. AJ was the first to speak.

"Come in, Vipond. Don't stand there like a whore waiting for her next customer."

"AJ, WITH ALL the attention you're getting, I figured I'd return for some more green."

"Vipond, I paid you a fair amount for what you did, and I have no intention of giving you a cent more for your trouble."

"You were his client?" I uttered those words while staring at AJ in disbelief, but I hadn't given much thought as to who was paying the cockroach.

"Don't gawp at me, Jake. Who else did you think would pay a private eye to carry out surveillance on a man like Elmo?"

She was right. Only a cockroach-shaped Vipond would have done her bidding for a handful of notes and no questions asked.

"AJ, if you're going to take that position, then you're putting me in an awkward situation." Vipond almost looked hurt as he spat out the statement.

"Vipond, don't be ridiculous. If you shoot me, then you'll get no more money. Be reasonable. If I throw you some green, will you go away?"

"You just said you wouldn't pay."

"Joss, the woman is a professional scam artist. She lies for a living. You can't believe a word she says. Of course, she'll contradict herself." He might not be the brightest star in the sky, but I figured I should help him understand the situation he was in.

"Shut up, Jake. You're only confusing him."

I fell silent because the barrel of the snub nose remained pointed at me, even though Vipond was the fella looking to shoot Avril Langchamp, a French woman with no past and possibly one husband or two. Or none.

"This is ridiculous." I yanked the wad of notes out of my pants pocket and threw some green at my shoes. "Joss, take your money and get out of here. Everything else is between me and AJ."

"Don't listen to him, Vipond. Look where he put your bonus: right by his feet. If you go over and collect, he'll have you in an armlock before you can shoot him between the eyes."

Joss took one step forward and then halted. AJ's words were having an effect. My gun burned a hole in its holster under my jacket, but I knew I wasn't fast enough on the draw to take both of them out in quick succession.

The sound of a car and its headlights flashed past the window. AJ shuffled toward the curtains and closed them, all the while keeping me in her sights.

"We don't need any of my neighbors getting involved in our discussions, now do we?"

—————

I DECIDED TO cut to the chase with AJ. "Assuming we find a way to get Joss some more gelt, why did you kill Kole? You've been so careful since you arrived in California. It's hard to believe you just snapped."

"Thanks to Vipond, I know you've been digging around, but how much have you found out?"

"AJ, I know about Warner, Kole and the Kennards, and the real estate deals you worked on with Julius."

Vipond's eyebrows appeared to be popping out of the top of his head. Either he underestimated me or AJ had spun him some yarn that he'd believed because she had paid him a bundle to not ask questions. And he had been dumb enough to comply. Now, he remained silent for a spell as he mulled over what he had learned.

"Then you know that the residential market was no longer workable for Julius and me." The snub nose shifted in AJ's hand as she spoke.

"You mean that Dragna had got wind of your scheme?"

"Not at all, Jake. Reselling the same apartment block only works when there's another sap willing to believe they can grab a deal that is too good to be true."

"You ran out of marks?"

"That's what I thought, but Julius reckoned there was always the next one just around the corner if we waited long enough. And I wanted to cut and run. The operation had been sweet for us, but we had to move on."

"So, how did he end up in that trailer park? It's not the kind of place you could take one of your marks."

"We'd hire office suites under false names when we needed them and had a home together in Malibu."

"Not in the trailer park?"

"No, that was where Julius would go after we rowed, when he was stewing. He'd spend a few days there and come back to me like nothing had happened."

"And is that where he is now? In your beachfront Malibu house?"

"How did you know it had a sea view, Jake?"

"A guess. If I was making sacks of cash, I'd dump it into real estate and give myself a comfortable life. What could be better than waking up and watching the waves hit the shore?"

"Nothing, Jake, unless you get greedy and have a vicious temper."

"AJ, you didn't answer my question. Is Julius hiding out in Malibu?"

"Of course he isn't, Jake. Listen to the woman. He's dead, right?" The cockroach had awoken from his reverie.

"Vipond is quite correct. On Sunday afternoon, I told Julius we needed to quit Malibu and find somewhere else to nest. He disagreed, and I ended up shooting him in the stomach."

"Did that kill him, AJ? It's a slow, painful way to go."

"That's why I put a second slug in his head."

I pondered for a moment.

"The same day you killed Kole. What was going on between the two of you?"

"For months, I could tell that Julius and I were over. He was getting more belligerent, and the real estate deals were clamming up. So, I set myself up in LA and found Kole Langchamp to do my dirty work. We made a big splash of our fake marriage, so we could embed ourselves in the local rich community and the next phase was to milk them for whatever we could get."

"And he had cold feet?"

"No, worse than that, Jake. He wanted more than his fair share. I'd offered him a fifty-fifty split on anything we made, but he got it into his head that he was the brains of the operation and deserved sixty percent."

"So you plugged Julius, drove over here, put Kole at his ease with a meal, and did for him in the evening."

"I figured if I pleaded diminished responsibility to the police over Kole, then they'd never link me to Julius's death if they ever found the body."

"You buried him?"

"Better than that, Jake. I took him in our boat and dumped him in the ocean. It'll be years before anyone discovers Julius's corpse."

A plaintive voice interrupted our conversation. "That's all very well, but what about me?"

41

WE BOTH TURNED our heads to stare at Joss Vipond.

"Although it would be wrong for me to speak on behalf of AJ, I'm guessing you've heard too much, Joss."

His left eye twitched and for a moment, Vipond's gun pointed at me and then pivoted back to AJ.

"You shut your mouth, Jake."

Her cheeks glowed red, and she held the butt of her snub nose ever tighter.

"Joss, you need to listen to me very carefully. If she shoots me, then you'll be next. This is a woman who wants it all and has shown she'll do whatever it takes to keep everything for herself."

A glance at AJ told me I was seconds away from being shot. I held my tongue and hoped my words had done enough to unsettle the man.

"All I want is my green and then I'll be out of here."

"Joss, it's at my feet. Come over here and collect it."

"I'm not that stupid, Jake. I've a better idea. You pick the green up and bring it over to me."

"Is that fine with you, AJ?"

"You bend down for that money and you'll never stand up again in your life."

"There's your answer, Joss. No can do."

I kicked a couple of the notes around my feet and then looked Joss square between the eyes. He blinked first.

"Why me, AJ?"

"What?"

"How did you end up choosing me for this caper?"

"I told you when we first met. Inspector Granger recommended you."

"Nothing more than that?"

"Nope. You were just an empty name to me."

"What about Joss?"

"I picked him out of the phone book. His offices were in an unpleasant part of the city, so I figured he'd be prepared to do more unsavory things to earn his pay. You came across as more upmarket, because a cop knew you."

"I'll take that as a compliment."

"If it makes you feel better. Men are all the same. Massage their egos and you've got them by the cajónes."

"Stop yacking and let's focus on my payment. That's the only reason I'm here."

"Joss, we're going in circles. There's cash here for you."

"But it's not from her. And however much chump change you walk around with, Jake, it ain't gonna be enough."

"Sounds like the man wants hush money, AJ."

I glanced back at AJ who continued to aim the pistol at me. I had hoped with all this conversation that she might have relaxed a little, but not this woman.

"He can whistle Dixie for that. I've already paid your fee, Vipond."

She spat his name out with disgust and he reacted the only way he knew. A slug spewed out of his gun and landed in the wall behind AJ. She tilted her head for a second and let a bullet fly out of her revolver.

Joss Vipond clutched his chest as a red circle formed on his shirt. He slumped to his knees as the circle became a river of blood and he collapsed, one leg twitching. I held out my hands, palms up, as AJ focused her attention on me.

"Should I see if he's alive?"

"What if he is? You know I'm going to have to finish him off. An intruder in my home that I've never seen before."

"Lou knows you hired me. You can't do the same to me."

"That is what keeps you in one piece right now. I might persuade the police that I shot one burglar, but even they aren't dumb enough to fall for two in an evening."

"Tell me, AJ. If you did for Kole yourself, what happened on Sunday night with Franny?"

"You met her. She was a crazy broad."

"Some of your neighbors reckoned they spotted her snooping around the house that night. Were they right?"

"When Kole popped upstairs, she appeared at the kitchen door, complaining that I was ruining Elmo's life. Half the time, I don't think she had a clue what she was saying."

"Was she right that your relationship with Kole threatened what was going on with Elmo?"

"Not at all. Kole was business and Elmo was pure pleasure."

"Fun enough to leave Julius for?"

"Don't be ridiculous. Julius was a man with a temper; Elmo was a boy with a taste for the good life. But he had no brains between his ears. We would never have a future together, despite what Franny believed."

"Wouldn't he have just faded away? Why did you have to kill him?"

"But I didn't, Jake. I had nothing against the lunk."

"So are you telling me that he committed suicide then?"

"That's not what I said. From what Franny was babbling, I wouldn't be surprised if she had done for Elmo and then killed herself. It's the sort of stupid thing she'd have got up to."

"Let me get this straight. You're telling me that Franny killed Elmo because he would never be happy with you?"

"Yeah, it sounds crazy because she was."

A whistle escaped my lips.

"Jake, all you had to do was a little digging to show the DA there was reasonable doubt that I'd killed Kole to give me my day in court, so that there was a legal record for any alibi I might have needed for Julius. If you'd poked around this house and found the documents

I'd left lying in wait for you, we could have had the whole thing wrapped up by Tuesday morning."

"AJ, this might be hard to believe, but I searched for papers and discovered bupkis. The only interesting item was in your trash, and that was a letter from Franny, which sent me on that wild goose chase."

She lowered the snub nose an inch as she took in what I'd said.

"The police must have taken the paperwork with them on Sunday night and ignored it when they dismissed my confession."

I shook my head in disbelief.

"Well, the game's over now, AJ. In a matter of minutes, the police will be here."

"You don't seriously expect me to believe that?"

"You think I'd have come here with no backup? Besides, Gladys Blake won't miss an opportunity like your two gunshots to call the cops and ask them to swing by."

With perfect timing, blue lights cast their beams between me and AJ on the living room wall through the crack in the curtains. In response, she pulled back the hammer on her snub nose and straightened her arm.

"You already told me there's no point in shooting me. It was true five minutes ago, and it's still the situation now."

"Don't con a con artist, Jake. We both know that you'll testify against me if you're alive."

"I'll hide behind client confidentiality. They'll get my name, rank, and serial number, but not much more."

"You are a material witness to a murder, Jake. There's no need to lie to me."

She glanced past the drapes for a second, but the snub nose didn't move from its position.

"Look, the cops are outside, and killing me won't change a single thing."

"It would make me happy, Jake."

"You won't last five minutes if you blow me away. Lou will come in all guns blazing and that'll be the end of you."

AJ glanced into the night again, and I knew this was my only chance. I could talk all I wanted, but she was right that she had nothing to lose. I flung myself at her and we both landed on the floor. With no time to spare—I hadn't got my gun out of its holster—I attempted to wrestle the snub nose out of her hands.

We rolled around on the floorboards. My head bumped against the couch and it hurt like there was no tomorrow. Then I got on top and twisted my body so that AJ landed with a thud back on the floor. Her head slammed against the wall and I hoped it had knocked her out, but no such luck.

She dug her nails into my hand and I screamed, but I was damned if I was going to let go. Then she was on top of me and we both had our hands on the gun, which was nestling next to our stomachs.

Before I knew what was happening, there was a thud, a flash, and intense heat on my belly. And a dampness there that I couldn't explain.

Then everything went black.

42

WHITE LIGHT BURNED into my eyes. I blinked several times, but it wouldn't go away. Perhaps this was heaven or my version of hell. I should have listened to the priests a bit more when I was a kid. I clamped my eyelids tight shut and hoped it'd vanish.

Voices. A man and a woman. I thought I recognized one of them, but couldn't be sure. When the heat of the lights faded and I no longer felt attacked by them, I opened an eye, then the other.

A woman in a uniform bent over me and prodded and poked until I complained. My stomach hurt like I'd gone ten rounds with Sugar Ray Robinson.

"How are you feeling, Mr. Adkins?"

"Call me Jake. All my friends do."

She scowled at me and waited for me to answer her question.

"My belly is pounding, but I'm fine apart from that."

Then a man's voice. "You are one lucky man, Jake."

Lou's face hove into view and I smiled.

"Good to see you too."

"When the shot went off, we came straight in and found you and Langchamp lying on the floor together, covered in blood."

"She shot me? You've got her in custody?"

"Don't be ridiculous. The gun fired and you fainted. She was the one who caught the slug."

"No kidding."

The nurse interrupted our conversation as she whipped off the bedclothes and replaced the bandages which were strapped around my middle. Lou retreated to the rear of the room to give me some privacy and pretended to read a newspaper.

When I was safely back under the bedsheets, he returned to my side.

"And did AJ survive?"

"Bled out on the way to the hospital."

We were silent for a spell.

"You're going to need to make a call to the coastguard, Lou."

"Oh?"

"The body of AJ's husband is lying at the bottom of the sea off Malibu somewhere."

"When were you planning on telling me this?"

"I found out this evening and if AJ hadn't tried to kill me, I reckon I'd have dropped a dime before the day was out."

He nodded. There was an edge of annoyance in his tone. After all, he was a cop, and I was not, and it looked like I knew more about his case than he did. To be fair, the district attorney had told him not to pursue the damn thing, but that didn't stop Lou from grinding his molars.

To take the sting out of the air, he walked to the foot of my bed and read my medical notes attached to a clipboard hanging near my feet. I strained my neck to glimpse what it said.

"Anything on there I should know about?"

"You've powder burns and nothing more, which is why you are in pain. That'll fade over the next few days. I'm sure the nurse will rub some lotion on it if you're lucky until they discharge you from this joint."

"Any idea when that will be?"

"When I spoke with your doctor, he wanted your bed as soon as you woke up, but I persuaded him to let you stay overnight. His bill is higher and you can receive some supervised rest. I know what you're like."

I smiled, knowing that Inspector Lou was correct. If I was at home, I'd hit a bar and try to get into all sorts of mischief. I owed

Sylvia a drink, for example. Being almost shot changes a fella's point of view of life.

"Tomorrow, you are going to have to come to the precinct as soon as you leave here and make a statement."

"I thought you might say that. The long and the short of it is this. AJ murdered Kole, who was not her actual spouse. She did this because they were involved in a real estate scam and he got greedy. Elmo Kennard was killed by his sister, Franny, who committed suicide. She was a nut job, who should have been in an asylum years ago. Then there's the small matter of Julius Warner, AJ's real husband, who she whacked in Malibu and dumped overboard from their boat."

"And you found out all this in one week."

"Don't blame me. Your DA put a deadline on this thing. If I'd had more time, AJ would probably still be alive."

"Always with the excuses, Jake."

AS PROMISED, ON Saturday morning, I left the hospital and wrote up my story for Inspector Lou Granger. With my help, the man had cleared four wrongful deaths in less than a week and the taxpayer would not spend a penny on any trials. I offered him the opportunity to take me for a celebratory drink, but he declined.

"Jake, let me do my job and you stick to taking photos of unfaithful husbands."

"That might pay very well, but it is not the only thing I do."

I breezed out of the precinct and popped two of the painkillers the doctor had prescribed me to help me get through the next week. He'd told me to expect some discomfort, and he wasn't kidding.

With nowhere else to go, I took refuge in the inner sanctum. Before I hopped into the elevator, I grabbed a copy of the Globe. A glance at the headline showed that Elliot had wasted no time after I left him the previous afternoon: Fraud Couple Dies in Dragna's Net. He'd got most of the details right and there was always Monday's correction to look forward to. And that should have been the day when the story hit the press. He'd promised me an embargo until midnight, but he hadn't specified which day. You never can trust reporters.

I limped into my office and slumped into my chair, regretting the action almost immediately, as I needed to stand up again to make myself a pot of coffee. Then an angel entered the room and deposited a mug in front of me.

"You are a godsend, Sylvia."

"Lou told me what had happened, and we figured you'd come here instead of going home like a normal person."

"You shouldn't talk to an invalid that way. I was involved in a life-or-death struggle yesterday evening."

"I've heard all about it. They found you lying on top of a dead woman. Did you get fresh with AJ and that's why she shot you?"

"There's no need to be mean, Sylvia. The doctor gave me medicine before I was released."

Sylvia hurried past the desk and put her arm around my shoulder.

"You poor thing. I should have known that Lou would act like you did nothing."

As she leaned into me, I noticed her scent and it smelled good.

"I still owe you a cocktail and I intend to repay that debt."

"You get better first, Jake."

Was she saying that because she wanted more than a drink from me, or was Sylvia's primary concern over my welfare? Either way, she was right. I wanted to be in bed early tonight. And by that, I meant alone with a hot water bottle and my meds.

Sylvia stood up and swanned back to her usual chair in front of me.

"Do you need a drink for your pills?"

"No, I'm good for now, thanks."

Then it struck me. The girl opposite was only interested in my well-being. She was loyal, honest, caring, and sexy. Curves in all the right places, which are all the things a man wants in a woman. I might have believed I'd died on Friday night and those pink pajamas sure were inviting, but no good would come of our sharing a bed.

Either she'd learn too much about me and leave because that's what many of my past lovers have done. Then I'd have no one to warm the sheets and need to find a new secretary. Or Sylvia would be just perfect for me, in which case you could bet your bottom dollar that I would get bored with her and I'd have to get a new secretary.

Neither of these options involved a happy ending. Both meant I'd be forced to place an ad in the paper. Sometimes the best thing is to be on a diet. You can look at the menu as much as you want, but it doesn't mean you have to taste anything.

"You might as well go home, Sylvia. There's nothing more for you to do here today."

"I could drive you to your apartment and make sure you're tucked up in bed for your convalescence."

"I'm good. Thanks all the same."

She bit her bottom lip and slunk out of the room. For my part, I spent two minutes trying to swing my feet up onto my desk so I could sit back and read the rest of Elliot's article. After much huffing and puffing, I made it and positioned myself with the newspaper lying on my lap and my coffee less than an arm's stretch away from my hand. Just how I liked it. Then I waited for the next client to come walking through my door.

I never found out who tried to run me over.

THANK YOU FOR READING!

Get a free novella

Building a relationship with my readers is the very best thing about writing. I send weekly newsletters with details of new releases, special offers and other bits of news relating to the Jake Adkins and Alex Cohen series, as well as information about my stand-alone novels.

And if you sign up to the mailing list, I'll send you a copy of the Alex Cohen prequel, The Broska Bruiser. Just go to www.leob.ws/signup and we'll take it from there.

Of course, if you prefer to jump right into the next Jake Adkins book in the series, then grab your copy of Habeas Corpus now.

And you can always follow me on BookBub if you want a quick and easy way to keep up-to-date with my work.

Enjoy this book? You can make a difference

Reviews are the most powerful tools in my arsenal when it comes to getting attention for my books. Much as I'd like to, I don't have the financial muscle of a New York publisher. I can't take out full page ads or put posters on the subway.

(Not yet, anyway).

But I do have something much more powerful and effective than that, and it's something that those publishers would kill to get their hands on.

A committed and loyal bunch of readers.

Honest reviews of my books help bring them to the attention of other readers.

If you've enjoyed this book I shall be very grateful if you would spend just five minutes leaving a review (it can be as short as you like) on the book's page. You can jump right to the page by clicking www.books2read.com/iconfess.

Thank you very much.

Leo

SNEAK PREVIEW

In Book 2, Habeas Corpus…

Thumping. I lay on my bed and wished I was dead. The throbbing in my forehead pounded at my skull like a horde of angry nuns attempting to escape my brain. Good rid of them, I thought, but they didn't take the hint and leave. I rolled onto my side and faced my nightstand. Someone had the foresight to leave me a glass of water and I consumed every drop, hoping the liquid would soak up all the pain in my cranium. No such luck.

The thumping repeated itself and I fancied that the noise might be some external phenomenon. As I swung my legs out of bed, I spotted myself in my wardrobe mirror. It was not a pretty sight. I lumbered toward the kitchen and flung some water in my face from the gurgling faucet. Then I meandered my way to the front door to find out what all the commotion was about.

I squinted through the peephole, but my eyesight was still too messed up to focus. There were shadowy figures; that was all I knew for sure. I opened the door to meet the satanic creatures who had awakened me from my deep slumber.

"Eamon. It's a bit early for house calls, sin't it?"

I caught sight of two flatfeet stood behind and either side of him and I corrected my language.

"I mean, Inspector Kavanah. To what do I owe this pleasure? I haven't had time to have breakfast."

He glanced at his watch, raised his eyes to heaven, and barged past me. With the two uniforms remaining in the corridor, I closed the door on them and followed Eamon into my living room. All my energy spent, I slumped into an armchair.

"What gives, Eamon?"

"We're searching for a missing girl."

"There's no one in my bedroom, but you are welcome to take a look. How old did you say she was?"

"She's legal. We're not talking about statutory rape, Jake."

He whipped out a photo from his notebook.

"Recognize her?"

I squinted at the picture. She was pretty,.

"I've never seen her before in my life."

"Her name is Sally Lyle, Jake. Take another look."

This time he passed the photograph to me and I looked again. She was still a stranger to me. I shook my head.

"Mind if I look around?"

"Be my guest. I'll be here when you get back from your tour."

A minute later and Eamon stood in front of me, a new level of seriousness on his face.

"You telling me you don't know Sally Lyle?"

"That's what I said just now, and that's still my position."

"So, what is she doing lying dead in your shower?"

To grab your copy, go to www.leob.ws/habeas.

OTHER BOOKS BY THE AUTHOR

Jake Adkins PI

The Case
I Confess (Book 1)
Habeas Corpus (Book 2–Due 2023)
Luther's Diamond (Book 3–Due 2024)

Alex Cohen

The Bowery Slugger (Book 1)
East Side Hustler (Book 2)
Midtown Huckster (Book 3)
Alex Cohen Books 1-3
Casino Chiseler (Book 4)
Cuban Heel (Book 5)
Hollywood Bilker (Book 6)
Alex Cohen Books 4-6
The Mensch (Book 7)

The Lagotti Family

The Heist (Book 1)
The Getaway (Book 2)
Powder (Book 3)
Mama's Gone (Book 4)
The Lagotti Family Complete Collection (Books 1-4)

All books are available from www.leob.ws and major eBook and
paperback sales platforms.

ABOUT THE AUTHOR

Leopold Borstinski is an independent author whose past careers have included financial journalism, business management of financial software companies, consulting and product sales and marketing, as well as teaching.

There is nothing he likes better so he does as much nothing as he possibly can. He has travelled extensively in Europe and the US and has visited Asia on several occasions. Leopold holds a Philosophy degree and tries not to drop it too often.

He lives near London and is married with one wife, one child and no pets.

Find out more at LeopoldBorstinski.com.

www.ingramcontent.com/pod-product-compliance
Lightning Source LLC
Chambersburg PA
CBHW031357250626
47155CB00004B/1309